FLYING TO THE FIRE

By Elyse Salpeter

This book is a work of fiction. The names, characters, places and incidents are products of the author's imagination. While certain places are real, the incidences regarding them are works of the author.

Amazon Edition

Edited by Denise Vitola
Published by Elyse Salpeter

Cover created by LLPix Photography

Dedication

This book is dedicated to Beth Ann Ryden, who believed in this novel and these characters enough to have me create a series. I'm indebted to her for giving me the chance to jump into the writing world.

I'd also like to thank my editor, Denise Vitola, who makes me look good, and my beta readers, Monica Rodriguez and John Steinmetz, who took the time to scour the novel for any changes. I appreciate all your help.

Finally, I'd like to thank the high school students at Mill Neck Manor School for the Deaf. They allowed me to pepper them with questions on the Deaf community and offered their own personal experiences so I could make this novel as accurate as possible. I truly appreciate all their help.

FLYING TO THE FIRE

Prologue

Seven and a half years ago, in a seaside villa off the coast of California...

The sound of the monitor whispered and hissed as the man slipped into the bedroom. The startled nurse rose from her chair and left. She was careful not to look him in the eye.

When he was sure he was alone, the man turned to the patient in the hospital bed and moved to her side. Now that he was closer, he could hear the sharp intake of her breath and see the way her chest rose and fell with each ragged breath. This wasn't supposed to happen to her. Not to his Marta.

She had once been so beautiful. Thick blond hair had brushed past her shoulders in soft curls and she had a regal, aquiline profile. She had reminded him of a queen who was supposed to stand by his side and rule the world with him. Now most of her hair had fallen out and her features were pinched with pain.

Marta slowly opened her eyes, those blue gems that most people thought were cold, but to him were fountains of pure, unadulterated beauty. "Samuel," she whispered.

He placed his hand on her forehead. Her skin was so brittle, his simple touch bruised her, and she winced. He quickly pulled his hand away. "I'm not going to let you go, Marta. That's unacceptable to me and I won't tolerate it."

She gave him a pitiful expression. "You have no choice. It's a wonder I've lasted this long. We both know that."

Samuel tried not to think about the accident. How one of his lab technicians had carelessly mixed up a quarantined experimental disease with a simple compound and brought it into the general lab where his wife had been working.

The moment the imbecile had uncorked it, Marta realized from the smell what had been released. She immediately put the facility on lockdown, even as the disease began to attack her vital organs. Emergency protocols were activated and the staff evacuated behind sealed doors. Only Samuel chose to break protocol, and equipped with the finest biohazard suit, had gone in to get Marta and bring her out, leaving his lab tech to die a torturous death on the floor of the lab room.

His team of scientists and doctors had worked feverishly to wipe out the effects of the disease on her system. Within days, the infection had run its course, but the damage to her body had been done. Her organs were permanently weakened and there was nothing any of them could do about it.

Or was there?

"Marta, I won't let death separate us."

"You speak in riddles, Samuel. Since when is death not the end?"

"I have a way to bring you back to me and it's based on the Anderson's theories. Let me tell you my idea." He leaned towards his wife's ear and whispered what he planned to do. Over and over again, day in and day out he repeated his plan, so that when she finally left this earth, the knowledge would remain in her subconscious. For he believed that death was not the final resting place and that her very soul and consciousness would still be alive. Somewhere.

He had to find the younger Anderson boy. The child knew about the afterlife and Samuel Herrington was determined to extract every single piece of information he could from him. His men were already on the hunt and it would only be a matter of time before he would learn what he needed to bring his wife back to this world.

But that never happened. A week later he was caught by the FBI, the boy got away, Marta died in a secret facility out east, and he was incarcerated for multiple lifetime sentences in Sing Sing. His plans had failed.

Or had they?

Chapter One

Seven and a half years later, in upstate New York...

It was the best thirteenth birthday present *ever*. The new bike was awesome. Much more awesome than the old one with the beat-up handlebars, chipped green paint, and ripped nylon seat. Danny pumped the pedals harder, feeling the gravel crunch under his feet. Michael had told him the sound resembled paper crumpling.

He'd have to take his word for it.

He'd had the bike for nearly six months, and he still marveled at how it performed, as if it had been designed especially for him. Gripping the handlebars, he jumped the curve and veered the bike onto the dirt path and into the woods. His calves burned as he raced through the fallen leaves. Wayward branches scratched at his cheeks, but he didn't care. He loved the feel of zooming through the forest and the freedom he felt when he was going so fast it was hard to breathe. Mostly, he loved the way it made him forget about things, like the nightmares he'd been having nearly every night--the one with the dark black twister that tried to suck the life out of him.

He shook his head to clear it and pumped harder, streaking along the path. He was glad his dad had put off-road tires on this one. He could feel the difference.

It was unseasonably chilly for late October, and his breath steamed in the air in front of him like a plume of smoke. Danny veered around a turn in the bend and was about to rush out of the woods and through Magnolia Fields when the air rippled in front of him and a huge black apparition like a tumultuous storm cloud appeared in his path.

With a yelp, he gripped the brakes on the handlebars too fast and flipped forwards headlong into and through the malignant mist, falling hard on the ground. His head crashed into a dead log. Thank God he had his helmet on. Stars covered his vision for a moment. The smell of decayed animals and rotted food overcame him, and he gagged violently. Sitting up, he felt a bitter coldness seep deep into his body. He gripped himself tight as the darkness closed in like a fog. He began to shiver and his fingers turned blue. Danny fell back to the ground and tried to catch his breath.

Little chunks flew out of the mass and hit his face. He realized they were bits and pieces of bugs and worms, some squirming onto his cheeks and others falling onto his arms and body. He started to fight, punching at the presence, but it was as if he were smacking against air. The pressure of this manifestation continued to get stronger and it physically pushed him to the earth as it forced its power against him. He could feel its energy and the way it was charging. Charging? That was impossible.

Danny's chest tightened as the mass pressed against it, crushing him bit by bit. He opened his mouth wide and screamed, hoping someone would hear him. With one last desperate attempt, he pulled into himself, felt the familiar electric push in his head and sent his thoughts upwards and out of his body. As he was about to black out from lack of air, he stared at the sky and that's when he finally saw them. They had heard his call and soared towards him. He felt profound relief, knowing he wasn't alone and that they would help him. In a fury of wings, a throng of birds descended and threw themselves into the black mass.

The mass released Danny to fight the birds and with the pressure gone, Danny turned over and wheezed and coughed violently. He tried to rise, but a wind picked up and threw him back to the ground again. The black mass spun and twisted itself into a spinning, whirling funnel. Danny was sucked into it as if he were in the path of a tornado. It dragged and whipped him through the dirt, his body flipping and turning in the brush until he was thrown against a small pine tree. He grabbed desperately at the low lying branches, ignoring the tears in his skin and the strain in his arms as the mass fought the birds, who again and again were flung out of the funnel, only to keep thrusting themselves back in.

A hummingbird was hurled at his feet. Its neck was broken and Danny tried to reach out to save it, but it was sucked back into the blackness, only to get thrown back to the ground repeatedly. Just before Danny thought he couldn't hold on any longer, the charges in the air changed and the mass retracted into itself and sucked back into the earth. The multitude of birds fell to the ground in a heap of wings with thuds so hard, he could feel them in his chest.

Danny crawled to them, touching each, one by one. Backs and wings broken, their necks twisted, he finally found one alive, laying within a mass of crushed insects. He cradled the quivering cardinal in his palms. Leaning down and whispering to it, the bird opened one of its black eyes, and stilled. A white light shot out of Danny's fingers and a shadow raced from his hands to the sky, disappearing into the clouds.

Danny turned to the other birds and, sniffling, gathered them together. He glanced into the woods, seeing shadows floating and bobbing in the trees. He shook his head sadly, knowing there was nothing he could do to help any of them. Placing the fallen birds in a pile, he covered them with a makeshift grave of dirt and leaves and said a little prayer. He looked at the forlorn shapes in the woods and with tears in his eyes, he nodded and watched as they disappeared into the trees.

Danny pulled up his battered, shaking body and grabbed his bike. He walked it out of the woods and into the field. Halfway through, he turned and saw the black hulking mass had returned, now teetering at the edge of the trees. It appeared to be watching him and it pulsated. Danny could feel the hairs on his arms stand up and could feel the energy of the beast as it was charging. How was it doing that? But then the mass collapsed into itself, oozing and spreading out like black oil, and with a ripple, sucked itself again into the ground.

Danny stood there trembling. He felt something wet tickle his cheek. He grabbed it with his hand, glanced at it and threw it to the ground.

It was a bloody, wiggling brown slug. He wiped his face with his shirt and saw a coat of slime covering his sleeve. With a shudder, he jumped onto his bike and hurried home.

The *thing* from his dream was no longer imaginary. The black mass was here and it was real.

And there was nothing he could do about it.

Chapter Two

Danny walked the bike to the side of the house and leaned it against the wall, hoping to get inside without being seen.

Not a shot.

As he was taking off his cracked helmet, Maddy Anderson poked her head out of the side door to ask him what he wanted for dinner, and with one look at her son, grabbed him and dragged him inside.

She sat him on a kitchen chair and helped him take off his filthy, muddy jacket, torn beyond repair. The shirt underneath was no better, with small rips and tears and large splatters of blood and gore. She leaned in and sniffed his neck, her nose crinkling in distaste and sat back, staring at him. Noticing the cuts on his face and the gashes on his hands, she waited over for him to start talking, but he wouldn't say a word. Finally, she signed in sign language to him. "Are you going to tell me what's going on?"

He shuddered, but remained silent, so instead she stood and got him a glass of water. He drank it down and shakily put the glass back on the table.

"Better?" she asked.

He nodded, but he still couldn't talk. Sighing, his mother grabbed some paper towels, wet them and started to wipe him down. She bit her lip as she gently cleaned his cheeks. He knew how hard this was for her. His mom was not a badgerer, but there was just so long she'd stay silent. He saw her staring intently at the dark rings under his eyes. She probably knew he wasn't sleeping well and having bad dreams, too. She most likely heard him calling out in his sleep.

She glanced at his hands. "Your fingers are bleeding. Let me go get the Bandaids," she signed. She went into the bathroom and came out with a medical kit. She opened it and proceeded to clean and bandage his wounds. "Is it those Malicky boys bothering you again? Because if it is, I'll have a talk with their mother."

Danny shook his head. He knew his mom didn't really believe it was them. She just wanted to fill the silence. "No, it wasn't them. I just fell in the woods," he signed. It wasn't a complete lie.

She arched her eyebrows, unconvinced. "You fell in the woods? And that's why you have cuts all over your body and smell like a garbage dump? And why there's a sticky green slime coating your face and clothes?"

He shrugged helplessly. He wanted to tell his mom what was happening, but he just couldn't. Not yet. She was super smart and brave and she knew about the birds. This was just completely different. This was bad and he didn't want her to get scared, at least not until he knew what he was actually dealing with. And he also didn't want her to think he was in trouble, or doing something like going crazy, because if she thought he could get hurt, she wouldn't let him go biking by himself anymore. Of course, if he kept coming home like this, she probably wouldn't let him go anywhere alone much longer anyway. With the mass out there, he wasn't so sure how brave he was going to be biking by himself either.

She pursed her lips. "Okay, Danny, but this conversation, or rather lack of conversation, isn't over." She stood up. "Go on upstairs and change your clothes. Daddy will be home late tonight, so we'll have to discuss this tomorrow." She touched his arm. "You know I'm always here for you, right? If you ever need to talk? We've been through some tough times before. I will do my best to listen and understand."

He smiled, hoping it seemed normal and would reassure her. "I know, Mom," he signed. "I'll be okay. And thanks." He ran upstairs before she tried to wiggle anything else out of him.

He fell onto his bed, reached onto his night table and grabbed his cellphone. He texted his older brother, Michael. Twenty-four years old and going to grad school in New York City, Danny always went to him when he had a problem. He understood him like no one else and never made fun of anything he said.

"Nightmares R coming again. Need help. U coming home?"

He waited on his bed, drumming his knee when the phone vibrated. "2Morrow. Got 1 week off for break. Can U wait?"

Yeah, he could wait. If he could just get through the night.

He replied to his brother and then went to stand by the open window. A gentle, feathery flick brushed against his cheek. "Please, not now," he thought with his mind, and with a flash, a shadow streaked out the window and left him blessedly alone. With a sigh, he shut the window, but not before he saw the trail of bugs slinking along the window's ledge. A steady stream of ants crawled up the sill, as if someone had left a trail of food. He flicked them away in disgust and slammed the window shut, trying not to think they were connected to the mass in the woods.

He changed his clothes and then lay down on his bed to wait for his mother to call him to dinner.

Chapter Three

The dream came again that night and it was just as bad as before, this time possibly even worse. The first time he'd had the nightmare about the mass was two years ago. It only came occasionally, but then over the past six months the dreams had been coming on with much more frequency. Now they happened nightly and he was starting to get scared to even go to bed.

Many times he'd wake up and he wouldn't remember his dreams, but his muscles would be all tense as if he'd just run a marathon, and his heart would be pounding so strongly he vaguely wondered if he were having a heart attack. Other times he'd remember everything in vivid detail. He'd wake and be gulping back bile as it threatened to rise from his stomach and choke him.

In the dreams, the evil always appeared as the black mass, but now it was escalating in its ferocity. And to know it was real and had transcended from just a dream to reality? He didn't know what it meant, and he was terrified of learning the truth because he didn't know how to fight against it. What would he have done if his birds hadn't come? He vaguely wondered if he really was going crazy. Dreams just didn't become reality, did they?

In this particular nightmare, it was summertime and he'd been skipping through Magnolia Fields towards the forest. The field was one of his favorite places in the world. It was so beautiful and picturesque. The meadow was covered with fragrant colorful wildflowers and little hillocks of low-lying bushes. He'd sit by small hidden pools and spend hours watching the frogs and lizards skip and jump. It was located just off the woods and Danny could never understand why no one hung out there more often. There was talk of putting a community park in, with a pool and playground, or even a walking path and benches, but politics and taxes always seemed to enter and the conversations simply stalled. Instead it was left wild, letting nature take its course and letting him have his own personal utopia.

The dream that night began the same way many of them did. He was sitting on a rock next to a stream with little birds skittering on the ground next to him. Something in the distance caught his eye and he noticed a group of little kids far across the field. They were running through the woods. It looked like they were playing tag and they reminded him of tiny fairies or elves the way they flit through the trees as if their feet never touched the ground. He started smiling because there was so much innocent happiness in their play and he wanted to be a part of it. He stood up, the little birds flying away, and began to run towards the children. Halfway across the field, fear overtook him as the horrible blackness appeared, surging from the earth behind the kids like a black tornado. Danny called out to them to watch out, to run and flee, but they didn't respond. He started running faster, trying to get close, but it was as if his legs were leaden, as if something were pressing on them to prevent him from helping and moving towards the children. Still, he pushed himself forward, feeling the strain in his muscles, begging them to respond, and they did, but slowly. He edged closer. He could now see the children signing to each other and realized that no matter how hard he screamed, they would never hear him. They were deaf, like him. Helpless, he watched the black mass advance, sneaking up on each child, one by one. Powerless, he watched it seep its evil onto each child, enveloping them and sucking them into its embrace. Though he couldn't hear, he could see the agony on their faces as the blackness consumed them, burning them one by one to crisps until all that was left on the ground were charred bodies.

Danny woke up with a scream stuck in his throat, his sheets twisted around him, and his body drenched in sweat. He sat by the edge of the bed until he could find his breath again. He had no idea why all of his bad dreams began in Magnolia Fields, because it was the one place in the world he always felt the safest. It reminded him of "the other place." The land he still wasn't allowed to talk about and tell the world it existed.

The place where souls went before they went on to heaven.

Danny knew he was different than other kids. There were things he knew that other people didn't. When he was a little boy, he figured out that birds really weren't what the rest of the world thought they were. They were really people, or people's souls, and that when humans died, their souls went into birds and they stayed there until they decided to move on and go to heaven. When Danny was six, an evil biophysicist, Samuel Herrington, kidnapped his parents because of that very knowledge. Danny's parents were scientists and had been double agents working for the United States Government, while Herrington actually thought they were working for him. Their cover job had been to work on experiments with light therapy and how it helped cure various diseases. But they had also worked on theoretical experiments having to do with bioethics and the afterlife, something near and dear to Samuel Herrington's heart. His wife Marta was dying at the time, and he wanted to know what was going to happen to her soul. When Herrington realized Maddy and Gary Anderson actually knew the answer and had withheld it from him, he kidnapped them. When he found out the knowledge was in their son Danny, he used all his resources to find him. It was then up to his older brother Michael to keep him safe. For the next week, they were on a run for their lives to find their parents and to escape from the maniac that hunted them.

And they had amazingly survived, but barely.

When it was all over, Danny's parents had sat him down.

"Danny, you can't tell anyone the truth about what happens to people when they die. You can never tell them people's souls go into birds and that you can send them up to heaven if they can't find their way. The world isn't ready for this kind of knowledge yet."

He had been so confused. "But why not? I can help them understand."

"We know, honey, but there are people who will not be able to accept what we have to tell them. Some people just can't handle the truth. It will scare them."

"But there's nothing to be scared about. They go to a happy place."

"We know, but you have to trust us on this. When you get a little older, we can talk about it more and then we believe you'll understand why we wanted to wait. One day you will be able to tell the world your amazing secret, but not just yet."

So he waited, but he hadn't understood. There had been more talk over the years with regards to religion and how the leaders of particular faiths around the world might take offense to what he wanted to share. That just because something is the truth, folks won't believe it because of faith and blind belief. It took Danny until he was nearly thirteen-years old to understand. He also realized there was a secondary issue even more dangerous than religious beliefs.

It wasn't that his parents didn't want other people to know the truth because they might dismiss it as heresy, but because they couldn't figure out a way to protect the birds if another evil person tried to control them. It wasn't just the actuality of starting a religious war around the globe, but a war on a person's very soul. If another like Herrington ended up figuring out which souls went into which birds, they would want to control them and then this person would have the power to control who would and who would not be able to go to heaven. They didn't want Danny to ever be used as a pawn for someone like that. Danny imagined humongous pens of caged birds. Hundreds of thousands of them with him standing there with a gun pointed at his head, telling whoever was in charge who were which birds. If the religious groups got their hands on him, they were afraid someone would use this information to try to force people to choose one religion over another. He imagined the Catholics against the Muslims, Jews against Baptists, and the Scientologists making everyone believe everyone really came from an alien species across the universe. So no, Danny's parents made him keep the secret so the knowledge would never get out until they could figure out how to keep everyone safe.

Now, seven years later, no one but their close inner circle and certain high-ranking members of the FBI knew the truth. The Andersons were still employed by the FBI and still studying anomalies having to do with the afterlife. And even with them working a hundred percent on figuring out a way to protect the birds, they were at a standstill in their research. Danny's ability to speak to the birds and to travel to the place that reminded him of Magnolia Fields only got him so far. In all the years since, he could never get past level fifteen. He traveled there occasionally but there was only so much those from above could tell him. He never actually got to see heaven, which he believed was one step above level fifteen. But level fifteen itself was a wondrous place. So peaceful and beautiful. He felt so safe in that realm. And when you were in the land, if you glanced straight up at the sky, a magnificent gem stretched across its heavens. There was an incredible energy emanating from that gem and the birds at level fifteen would take themselves up and into that gem and then would simply disappear. Danny could only assume it was the ultimate place, the version of heaven every religion touted.

And he had tried to go there. In fact, he had tried a whole lot of times. Once, when he was ten, he let it slip to his mother he'd tried to move into the gem and she'd been horrified.

"What do you mean you tried to go up into the gem? Didn't we tell you never to do that? It could be dangerous."

"But I wanted to see what it was like up there."

"Honey, I know, but what if you went into the gem and disappeared? What if you couldn't come back down? How would we ever get you back?" His mother had been close to tears.

"Are you scared of heaven, Mom?" He'd been so confused by her fear.

She had held him and hugged him hard. "Maybe I'm a little scared, Danny. We don't know exactly what heaven is and we don't know what really happens to us when we get there. I know you're getting older and I know when you're there in that land I can't control you and tell you what to do, but I need you to listen to me and please, don't try to go up any higher. Not until we learn more. I would be so upset if I lost you."

"It's okay, Mom. I don't think I can go up even if I want to. When I pushed myself higher, it was as if I were stopped by a force field or something, like in the science fiction movies. My body would rise and it was almost like I was touching an invisible rubber band that would let me move a little bit ahead, but then would push me back really hard."

She had stared at him, the scientist in her winning out over her parental instinct. "So this field won't let you go further up?"

He shook his head. "One of the birds told me it's because I'm still alive. Only when I'm supposed to go, will I be able to."

That had mollified his mother enough to stop squeezing him.

But, while he couldn't get past level fifteen, his powers had grown significantly. His mother worked with him diligently for years until he was able to take over his studies on his own. Now, just by thinking about it, he could call birds to him at will without the aid of the machine. His mother had created the machine when he was younger to help him channel his powers and make them grow. Now Danny was so skilled, he didn't need to use it at all. He could do things all on his own. He could hear them in his mind at all times if he wished. He could speak to them and reach out to them for help. But his powers didn't stop there. He could travel to level fifteen whenever he wished and he learned how to channel that ability and take his brother and parents there whenever he wanted.

Now that he was older and more skilled, he knew "the how and why" of his abilities and could do it whenever he wished. He was able to channel this special area of his brain where he could generate a power--a rustle in his mind that would change the electromagnetic energy in the air around him. He could then literally see their auras and he'd latch onto them, grabbing them and taking them away with him.

He remembered the time when he was eight and he'd taken his mom back there. It was the first time she had returned to that land in two years.

Danny sat on the floor of his mother's lab, playing with his ability. The window was open and as his mother took notes, Danny called birds to him. All sorts of species came through the window, different people from all sorts of lives, telling them their stories, their hopes and dreams and their fear of the above. Danny did his best to calm each of them and assure them where they were going was a safe place. Some he even helped get there by sending them to the light with his powers if they were unable to get there on their own.

One particular bird kept coming back. It was a little boy who had passed on from an illness the year before. He was scared and asked Danny if he would come with him. Danny told him he would take him right to the gem and his mother's eyes widened in fear when she saw what Danny signed to the little bird. He didn't have to sign to the birds to speak to them, because he could hear them in his head, but his mother had asked him to sign to them so she could understand what was happening while he trained with her.

"Danny, you can't take him to the gem. You can't go that far with him."

"Mom, it's okay."

"No, it's not okay. We don't know what that place is."

The little bird suggested he bring his mom along so she wouldn't be worried. So, with a mischievous smile on his face, Danny searched for the special place in his head to make the rustles and before Maddy could even say a word in protest, she collapsed onto the floor right next to her unconscious son and the now inert bird.

It was a good thing Gary had been monitoring them from the next room or he would have had a heart attack seeing Maddy and Danny suddenly slumped on the floor of the lab, apparently dead. He raced into the room and checked their pulses with his stethoscope, detecting the slightest of heartbeats. He knew now what had happened, but could do nothing about it but wait with them until they woke up.

And when they woke up, Maddy immersed herself at her computer for hours recording what she had felt and seen.

Danny was just happy to have been given the chance to play with the little boy a bit more before he moved on to the light.

So Danny continued to work on his abilities and learned how to harness his energy to seek out souls and "grab them," taking them with him whenever he wanted.

He'd bring his family and once even Mr. Daley, the FBI agent who helped them all those years ago, to level fifteen. They could walk around the beautiful fields, explore the mountains, but most of the time, the people he took simply spent their time staring at the humongous gem above their heads and basking in its glow. In Maddy's reports, she explained the feelings at level fifteen were equivalent to a full-fledged emotional high. When you were there, your body went into a euphoric state and you so badly wanted to stay there it took everything in your power to allow Danny to take you back down. And take her down he did. With a gentle pull on her being, Maddy described it as a gut wrenching tug deep inside her, whisking her away from unreality to the cold hard reality of this existence. You even went into a mini withdrawal of sorts, almost a deep depression, but thankfully, the feeling lessened with each passing second you were back in this world.

So, until his parents and the FBI figured out a way to let the world in on this big secret and figured out a way to protect everyone, he went back to being just a regular kid and had to keep this most magnificent of truths a secret.

Danny saw a dark reflection in his mirror and turned to the window. A large black vulture stood on the sill, blocking the moonlight. With a shaky smile and jelly legs, Danny moved over and opened the window up. The bird hopped into the room and spread its wings in a hello. There were crusted blood stains on its beak and Danny could see a cut healing on its belly.

Concerned, Danny put out his hand and stroked the head of the bird sending it a message in his mind.

"Are you okay, Dr. Polensky? What happened to you?"

Dr. Polensky was Danny's old pediatrician, aka Mr. FBI secret spy agent, who had been assigned to watch out for Danny ever since he was born. He had died three years ago at the ripe old age of eighty from a massive heart attack and simply decided not to move on to the light, choosing instead to stay around. Danny had a feeling he was officially still working his case and refused to let it go. Occasionally, Danny tried to link to Dr. Polensky's soul to try convince him to move on, but the doctor adamantly refused and pushed him away each time. Danny could tell he meant it, that he wasn't ready to move on, so he'd eventually leave him be. He knew he could force it on him and send him against his will, but it wasn't how Danny used his powers, and at thirteen-and-a-half years old, even he understood the magnitude of taking someone's soul against their will. But even though most secrets were no longer kept from him, Danny was sure Dr. Polenksy had a few of his own he kept close. He also seemed to have an uncanny sense of when Danny had a bad night and would suddenly show up in his room.

"Oh, I'm okay, Danny. Just got into a bit of a scrape the other day. Nothing I can't handle. So, tell me what's going on. I saw something happen to the birds in the woods outside of Magnolia Fields and there are other things going on as well. I think you might have an idea what it is. Something's changed in the atmosphere as if a storm is brewing, but it feels all wrong. Do you know what it is? Or what even happened to those birds?"

Danny swallowed hard. *"The blackness got them, Dr. Polensky. It attacked me in the woods when I was biking home and then attacked the birds when they came to help me."*

The bird twitted. *"The blackness attacked you? This is the same blackness from your dreams you're speaking about?"*

Danny nodded. *"Yes, it's the exact same one and I'm dreaming about it nearly every night now. But, it's not just a nightmare anymore. It's real and it has broken through to this reality. Do you know what it is?"*

Dr. Polensky didn't answer right away.

Danny shook his head, a tear running down his face. *"When the blackness killed those birds there was nothing I could do for them. It slaughtered them right in front of me. I could only save just one soul."*

Dr. Polensky hopped around the room and then flew up to Danny's dresser, turning his head to eye a photo of Danny and his family. *"Those people knew what the consequences were when they flew down to help you. What came for them was beyond your control or our understanding at this time. You weren't responsible for their deaths. You need to understand and accept that."*

Danny brushed the tears away fiercely. *"How can you say that? Of course, I'm responsible. They came to protect me and died for me. Now they're just going to be lost forever."*

The bird stared at him, cocking its head. *"Danny, death is not the final resting place. You know that by now, don't you? They'll come back eventually and find their way. It will just take time."*

Danny gazed at his toes, wiggling them. He knew Dr. Polensky was right. Danny and his family had spent years and years studying so many religions and their beliefs in the afterlife. It all came down to one central idea anyway in his mind. Life on this plane was meant to be lived now and when we died, it wasn't the end. No matter which religion you studied your existence wasn't just over. Some folks believed in heaven, some believed in reincarnation, some believed in other even more obscure things like an overriding energy controlling things. But in the end, life in some capacity, continued. Even if the belief was that your essence simply lingered on in the atmosphere, like when a flame from a candle is snuffed out and the wisps of smoke join and comingle with the air, you will still exist in some fashion. Danny knew that a heaven, or one he called heaven, was real. But what was it really? He didn't know, because no one could tell him what was in that gem floating above them all.

But what he did know was that those birds who died in the woods wouldn't be doing much of anything for a very long time. If he couldn't send them on to the light and they were killed in a bird body, they were simply going to roam this plane of existence until some overriding power allowed them to move on. He just knew it would seem like forever for those lost souls.

Finally Danny looked up, realizing something. *"But, Dr. Polensky, if we agree death isn't the final place and heaven is not the end place, then what else is there? What is this thing forcing its way into this world?"*

"That's a good question, and one I think you've already figured out." Dr. Polensky stared at him with such an odd expression that Danny's mind finally turned to a place he hadn't wanted to consider. He remembered the black mass shooting back down into the earth. The coldness it brought; the smell of rotting flesh. The bugs and worms spewing from the ground. Yes, there were other places besides earth, level fifteen and heaven. There were other places besides the beauty of Magnolia Fields. There were other places that didn't just go "up." Evil places steeped in agony, bottomless pits of despair, places of suffering and torment. Places where boogiemen and nightmares came from.

"No, that's not possible," Danny said.

The bird stared at him with its black eyes. *"Isn't it? Who said beings only go up?"*

Danny closed his eyes, his skin breaking out in goose bumps. People talked of places where murderers and evil people went when they died. Heck, most religions had a name for that place. But Danny had no physical knowledge of its existence. When a bad person died in a bird body, their soul simply disappeared. He couldn't feel it or latch on to it if he tried. Their entire essence just vanished, so in his mind he felt like they all just ceased to exist. But what if that wasn't true? What if their soul really did go somewhere?

He nodded, realizing Dr. Polensky was correct. He did know where the black mass was coming from. It was coming from the very opposite of heaven. It was coming from the muck. Coming from deep in the black earth. Down…

He gulped, not even wanting to say the word.

Chapter Four

The morning brought sunlight and the welcoming smell of pancakes and bacon. Danny squinted, rubbed his face and shuffled to the bathroom. Not even bothering to do more than what needed to be done, he bypassed the sink and groggily moved down the stairs, letting the smells from the kitchen propel him on.

At the bottom of the steps, he bumped into a big blue suitcase with a New York University sticker on it. That meant only one thing and he woke up quickly. Michael was home. Elated and grinning ear-to-ear, Danny raced into the kitchen, ready to pounce on his brother, but then stopped dead in his tracks when he entered the kitchen. Michael wasn't sitting at the kitchen table shoving his face into a stack of pancakes with his laundry piled in heaps around him and his mom touching his face as if she hadn't seen him in years. Nor was he sitting there debating with his father about some biophysical, scientific mechanical doohickey they always yammered on and on about as if it were the most important thing in the world. He also wasn't sitting there waiting for Danny to finally wake up to do some crazy joke on him, like put a rubber spider in his orange juice or a whoopee cushion on his seat, or just tackle him to the floor, which was his normal mode for greeting him, complete with a noogie to the head.

No, instead he was seated at the kitchen table, an actual fork in his hand and speaking to a girl sitting next to him. He even looked different, as if he had shaved and put on real clothes instead of the ripped jeans and concert t-shirts he wore all the time.

Danny stood there, not knowing quite what to do and watched as the girl laughed at something Michael said and playfully smacked him on his arm.

Michael grinned and glanced up, seeing Danny. His smile was genuine. "Hey, Birdman. You're finally awake," he signed.

Danny scowled. He hated that nickname Michael had given him all those years ago. It reminded him of Big Bird from Sesame Street every time he said it. "It's Danny."

"Oh, don't be so sensitive." Michael jumped out of his seat and grabbed Danny in a big bear hug and Danny couldn't believe he actually smelled cologne on him, too. "Fine, Danny it is. Hey, come on over here, I want you to meet someone."

Michael brought Danny over to the girl, who now smiled at him. He was suddenly shy and more than a little embarrassed, realizing he wore an old ripped Spiderman t-shirt a size too small and dirty sweatpants that had ice-cream stains with chocolate sauce on them from the night before. He tried to pat his hair down, but felt it spring back up.

"Hi," he said out loud, trying to pull his shirt down over his stomach.

The girl signed to him. "Hi back, Danny." She was really pretty, with light blue eyes and blond hair. It was so curly it seemed if you grabbed one of the curls and pulled it and then let it go, he'd bet his Derek Jeter Rookie card it would spring up and bounce around her head like a jack-in-the box. Her skin was really pale, like she never went out in the sun and her smile was wide with super white teeth like you saw in toothpaste television commercials. "It's really nice to meet you. Michael's told me all about you."

Michael beamed at the girl. "This is Charity. She goes to grad school with me. And guess what? She knows ASL. How cool is that? She took it for fun for a few years as an undergrad for her language requirement."

Danny crinkled his nose. "You met her at school? In the labs with all that gear on you said you wear?" He was thinking of the Hazmat suits that covered you from head-to-toe that Michael told him he had to wear all the time from all the dangerous experiments he was working on.

Michael grinned. "Well no, not in the lab. We actually met on the street corner outside the biochemistry building."

Charity chimed in quickly. Danny could see her giggling from the way her shoulder's bounced. He read her lips. "Yeah, when you went barreling headlong into me because your head was stuck in your iPhone texting away. You nearly made me drop my latte. Those things are expensive."

Michael mocked being shocked and laughed. "Oh, really, like you weren't totally engrossed, singing away on your iPod. People could hear you down the block. You didn't even see me coming."

The two of them started laughing and Danny felt like a third wheel. He sat down at the table and grabbed a strip of bacon on a serving plate in front of him and took a bite, determined to ignore them both until he could process his brother with a girlfriend. Here in his own house. The last time Michael dated someone was over a year ago and Danny hadn't even met that girl.

As he was munching, Danny's father came into the room, his arms heavy with grocery bags. "Michael, did you forget I was outside in the driveway getting the groceries? Could have used your help, buddy." Danny was pretty sure his tone was sarcastic.

"Oh, I'll help, Mr. Anderson. Here, let me take that." Charity jumped over to him and grabbed a bag from him.

"Well, thank you. Nice to see someone around here with manners. God forbid my boys get up. You must be Charity. It's so nice to finally meet you." He put down the bags and shook her hand as Maddy Anderson came up from the basement, a gallon of both orange juice and milk in her hands and a seven-year-old quick at her heels.

"Ah, good, you're finally back, Gary." She handed the containers to Michael who put them on the kitchen table and glanced at her daughter, nodding in the direction of the dinette. "Katie, honey, please go take a seat."

Michael whisked the little girl in his arms and planted a huge kiss on her cheek. She squished her face and squealed as Michael plopped her in her chair.

Maddy turned to Danny, signing. "Good to finally see you up, young man." She eyed his clothes and raised her eyebrows.

He shrugged, but what was he going to do? Run upstairs and change? A little late for that now.

His mother moved to the stove and started making stacks of pancakes. "So, Charity, what year are you in?"

"Just my first year, but we've done so much in just two months. I feel like I've been there forever already."

Maddy nodded. "Working in a lab can do that to you. What were you doing before?"

Charity accepted a cup of coffee from Michael, smiling adoringly as if he had picked the beans himself, and then turned back to his mother. "After I graduated with my Bachelor of Science degree from Stanford, I was hired to work on the west coast at a pharmaceutical company. I thought it would be exciting, but basically I was just a glorified bean counter, sectioning out medications and pills for generic drugs. That's not what I went to school for. I want to get my hands dirty and start doing something more than just dealing with the bureaucratic issues of politics and medical companies. So, I applied and started grad school at NYU to advance my degree."

Gary sat down at the table. "So what is it you specialize in, again? Michael said something about entomology studies. You know, I've always had a strange passing interest in insects. Katie here loves them." He took a plate of pancakes from Maddy and placed them on the table.

"Dad, it's not just studying about plain old bugs, but molecular biology studies at the cellular and genetic levels," Michael answered. He started signing again. "She'll be studying the same theories that I do, but with an emphasis on insects and worms. She's conducting these amazingly intricate bioelectromagnetic experiments to fight autoimmune disorders."

Charity took a sip of orange juice and leaned forwards. "He makes it sound so exciting, but we all know I take classes just like everyone else and sit in a lab with a bunch of other drones playing with terrariums and watching how insects interact. Though I do like saying I'm a bit of an oligochaetologist mixed with a side of entomology. I think it sounds cool, doesn't it?" She grinned at Danny.

Gary cocked his head. "Bioelectromagnetic experiments fighting autoimmune disorders on a cellular and genetic level. Gee, Michael, you seem to know a lot about this field of study. I don't recall you taking any of these as prerequisites on your schedules in school these past few years."

Danny watched Michael's face redden while he grabbed the syrup and busied himself pouring.

Charity smiled at Michael and gently touched his arm. "You know, your son is just brilliant and eats up everything I tell him. I swear he might be coming over to the dark side if he keeps hanging out in my lab. Everyone thinks he's trying to steal my notes the way he's been showing up all the time. I might have to talk to my lead to see if there's an opening in the department."

Michael raised his eyebrows, seemingly getting his composure back. "Oh, right, like you haven't been stalking me on my own stuff, too? Everyone in the lab is talking about us, you know."

Charity raised her eyes. "Really? Like I could actually use any of your notes on embryonic patterning and the control of gene expressions in humans for my research. Maybe you should stop buying me coffee every morning and leaving little gifts around the lab for me to find and people will finally stop talking." She grinned as she fingered a red scarf around her neck that when Danny looked closer had little tiny ant designs on them. "But I do love it."

Maddy laughed and sat down, putting another platter of pancakes on the table. "They sound just like us when we first met, don't they Gary?"

He nodded. "Yes, they certainly do, but without the bugs."

Danny shook his head, exasperated at watching the entire exchange. "You know what? I think you're all crazy." He started eyeing his sister who was acting completely out of character and for once wasn't trying to be the center of attention. She stared intently at something in her lap, and his stomach convulsed when she picked it up and held the object, clearly alive and wiggling, in her hands. It was a huge bug that resembled a cockroach, but this one had this weird black mark on the top of its body.

Katie stared at it, as if mesmerized, holding it upside down as the legs flicked and wiggled in the air. He knew she wasn't scared of it. For God's sake, she acted like a boy half the time, playing in the dirt and exploring ant hills. The grosser the bug, the better in her book. He remembered their parents once taking them to a poisonous spider exhibit at the museum and while all the other girls and their moms screamed and hid behind their hands, Katie had her face literally plastered to the plate glass terrariums and would've stayed for hours if their mom hadn't finally moved them along. Katie kept saying they were hungry and no one was taking care of them properly. She actually threw a huge tantrum and he remembered his mother making a nice little cash donation right then and there, basically begging the staff to feed the darned bugs so she could get Katie to finally leave. And they did leave, but not until Katie saw every cage get something to eat. Crazy.

Charity leaned forward, her eyes wide with surprise. "Hey, will you look at that? It's a *Blaberus craniifer*." She fingerspelled it and then turned to Michael. "Why didn't you tell me Katie keeps these little guys as pets? I would have brought her one."

"Because she doesn't keep them as pets," Maddy exclaimed quickly. Her face puckered in disgust. "What in the world is that thing?"

Charity shrugged, like it was no big deal. "It's just a death's head cockroach, which is called that mostly because of the markings on its thorax. See that black mark up there?" She pointed at the top of the bug's body. "It's pretty tame for the most part and keeps really well as a pet, though I have to say, this one is really big. In fact, I'm kind of surprised to see it here in your house wild in the first place. But, regardless, I wouldn't worry about her playing with it, Mrs. Anderson. It's not dangerous at all."

Maddy huffed. "Maybe not, but it certainly doesn't belong at my kitchen table."

Katie leaned forward and brought the creature to her face. She squinted and then leaned in and sniffed the wiggling, writhing creature.

"Katie, come on, give me that. It's kind of disgusting. No offense, Charity." Michael reached for Katie's hand, but she clutched it and waved it out of his reach. Katie glanced at Danny and an unspoken message went between them. In that second, everything felt all wrong for him, like something bad was going to happen. His stomach flip-flopped and the pancake he was chewing suddenly tasted terrible. He glanced at Katie, but her face had crinkled up as if she were about to cry. Without any warning, she slammed the creature hard on the table and squished it on the tablecloth, its guts and overturned milk and coffee cups splattering everywhere.

Everything happened fast. His mother jumped up as a whole glass of milk landed in her lap, his father grabbed at his daughter to get her hands off the dead insect and Michael and Charity grasped at napkins and tried to clean up the spills.

But Danny was frozen. He stared at his sister, who was now glancing outside, her bottom lip quivering. She looked out towards the woods, then the ground and he realized she knew. Knew something bad was happening. His heart filled with dread and he excused himself from the table and ran upstairs, his breakfast forgotten.

It wasn't Michael he was going to have to talk to at all now. He didn't know anything except how to stare at his new girlfriend and make gaga faces.

He was going to havc to talk to his sister.

She knew.

Chapter Five

After the debacle in the kitchen, things went back to some semblance of normalcy. Once everything was cleaned up, Michael glued himself to Charity's side to watch a movie in his bedroom, his parents immersed themselves in their home office finishing up some reports for the lab, and Danny had been given the task to watch his sister. This was probably the first time he actually didn't mind.

He found her in the den. She had the captions on while watching the cartoons and loved reading along while the show was on.

He wondered how to begin. She was just a little kid, so how much could she possibly tell him? But then again, hadn't he been younger when he found out about all his abilities and what they meant? He realized that back then, Michael must have been in the same boat as he was right now, trying to get answers about the afterlife from a six-year old. He bet it hadn't been easy.

He turned off the television against her protests and started signing to her. "Katie, I have to talk to you about something."

She jumped on top of him playfully, but he put her back down on the couch. "Not now. I have to ask you a question. Is there something going on you want to tell me?"

She just stared at him confused, and he realized he'd have to be more specific. He had an idea. "Have you been having bad dreams at night?"

Her eyes widened a little and she nodded. Bingo. He realized if he hadn't asked, he'd have no idea if she was having bad dreams or not because he couldn't hear her at night if she ended up calling their mom. He peered at her closely, noticing the same dark circles under her eyes as his, realizing how quiet she'd been recently, always right at his mother's heels. He felt guilty and suddenly very protective of his little sister. A first for him. To be honest, he'd never really given her much thought, thinking her more of an annoyance than anything else.

He'd been shocked when his parents had sat Michael and him down and told them his mother was pregnant. It had been a month since they had escaped from Herrington and his mother had spent a lot of that time recuperating from her ordeal. Who knew she had already been four months pregnant? Danny had been badgering her for years about having another baby, but when push came to shove, he suddenly imagined what it would be like having all the attention taken away from him. They had been at the kitchen table, and they'd just served him a huge ice-cream sundae before dinner. He should have known something was up before they even blurted it out. Pregnant? His mom was already forty-three years old at the time. He didn't even think people that old could even have babies anymore. He remembered his mother telling him.

"It's as much a surprise to us as it is to you guys," his mother said. "For the past few months I had thought I'd just been tired from working long hours at the lab. And now, to know I was pregnant and the baby is okay after everything that happened to us? We're just so incredibly happy she's healthy."

"She?" he asked. A girl? He'd wanted a baby brother. A girl baby never entered his mind.

His mom smiled. "That's right, Danny, you're going to have a baby sister. Isn't it wonderful?"

But no, it hadn't been wonderful and he hadn't jumped on board the happy express like the rest of them had. Suddenly there was a baby in the house grabbing his things, drooling all the time and taking all the attention away from him. So what that he knew about the afterlife and what happened to you when you died? So what that he had just survived a cross-country chase from the most evil man on the planet? So what that he could talk to birds? So what that he was deaf? Apparently, it was nothing compared to a fat-cheeked, pooping, puking, and burping little baby with pink bows fastened in her one fat curl, bouncing on your lap.

It wasn't like Michael was any help either. He was leaving for his first year of college soon, letting Danny deal with his annoying sister all alone.

Katie had come into the world a month early, but healthy and he'd just had to adjust.

As Danny stared at her, he smiled. Katie definitely wasn't a fat, burping, annoying little baby anymore. She was actually kind of cute with big brown eyes and straight light brown hair she wore in two braids down her back. She didn't run around like a dopey little girl either. She was a tomboy and would beg him to throw a ball with her in the backyard if their father wasn't around, and she was always climbing on things and getting dirty. His mother was constantly changing her clothes and patching her blue jeans. He also didn't know too many girls who preferred getting a football versus a princess outfit at her age for their birthdays. All of his friends' younger sisters were worried about their pretty dresses, their baby dolls and what color their fingernails should be. He didn't remember Katie ever letting his mom paint her fingernails, now that he thought about it. Well, maybe once. She went to one of those girly birthday spa parties and they put a special nail polish on that made her fingernails look like cracks and spider webs. She had liked that.

"So, want to tell me about your dreams?"

Her eyes got teary and her face crumpled. "No. They're really scary," she signed. Her signing was strong and between reading her lips and her signing, he could understand her perfectly. He silently thanked his parents for making the entire family learn sign language so he could communicate with them. So many of his other friends who were deaf weren't so lucky. Most of them were forced to write everything down all the time in order to convey their needs. He couldn't imagine having to do that every moment of every day, just when he needed to ask something as simple as what was for dinner, help with his homework or if he could he have his allowance.

He patted Katie's arm. "Hey, I can handle it. Try me. Maybe it will make you feel better."

She picked at a new hole on the knee of her jeans and then glanced up, signing. "I keep dreaming about bugs. But they're not the cool bugs like the ones I like to play with. These are huge and dirty and smelly. And they keep trying to talk to me."

This startled him. "What do you mean they talk to you? In the dreams they're talking to you and you can understand them?"

She nodded. "Yeah, but I don't just talk to bugs in my dreams." She stopped and picked further at the hole in her jeans again, clearly stalling.

He touched her hand, and she looked up. "Katie, tell me," he spoke.

She stared at him. "They talk to me all the time. Even when I'm awake."

He got chills. Was it possible? Could she actually communicate with bugs the same way he communicated with birds? Why didn't anyone in the family know about this? "Katie," he signed. "You understand insects? It's not like they're your pets or something and you just really like them and understand what they need?"

She cocked her head, clearly thinking about how to explain herself. "It's not like that. When I'm awake, the bugs don't speak with words, but I do know what they're feeling. But the ones in my dreams can speak, and they say really bad, scary things and show me stuff."

"What do they show you?"

Her lips quivered. "They show me dead things and scary places. And creepy people." Her eyes welled up, and she swiped at them.

"Creepy people?"

She bit her lip. "Yeah, all these people, crying and screaming and moving around like this." She stood up and hunched her back over and started lurching. It reminded him a little like a gorilla or the Disney movie with the hunchback in *The Hunchback of Notre Dame*. "The bugs tell me the people are going to come get me and eat me. That they need me for something." She teared up.

"It's okay, we don't have to talk about those creepy people and the scary dreams right now." His thoughts brought him back to breakfast. "Can you tell me what happened in the kitchen this morning? Why did you kill that cockroach? I thought you loved those things."

"It wasn't like the regular ones. This one was like the ones in my dreams. It was whispering to me bad things and it smelled bad, too. Couldn't you tell?" She stopped talking and spun around and he turned around to see what she was now looking at.

Michael and Charity had come into the room. Charity plopped herself on the couch right next to them, crisscrossing her legs. Charity nudged Katie in her side, oblivious to their conversation. "I think it's incredibly cool how much you like insects. Did you know, I'm the only girl in the lab who's not freaked out by them? We girls have to stick together. Here, I have something for you." She had her pocketbook slung over her shoulder. One of those huge bags, which had a gazillion zippers. Danny never knew how girls found anything in them.

Charity opened the big center zipper and pulled out an oversized picture book with dog-eared pages. It was a color photograph book on insects. She handed it to Katie. "After Michael told me how similar we were, I thought you might like this. I've had it ever since I was a little girl and it was my very favorite book. My daddy gave it to me when I was just a little older than you." She glanced at Danny. "I know. It's weird for a girl to like bugs so much. Right? But, I always had a fascination with them. As I got older it just sort of morphed into worms and flying species and anything that had to remotely do with them. Put extra legs and some wings on them and I'm golden." She turned back to Katie. "Now I'm studying to be a scientist and I'll get paid to study and play with them all day long, which I think is pretty cool."

Danny watched, fascinated as her curls bobbed up and down on her shoulders as she talked. Like little springs.

Katie took the book in her lap and gingerly opened it up. Her eyes widened and she started smiling and Danny knew she'd be engrossed for hours. Charity dove back into her bag, in one of the side zippers, and brought out a small plastic case. She reached inside and pulled out a chain link necklace with a small golden pendant on it. She turned to Danny, her expression a little embarrassed. "I know it's strange I'd get you something when you don't even know me, but Michael told me how much you like birds, and I remembered it when I was in this little crafts shop near the university the other day. They make all kinds of neat things and it just sort of jumped out at me. I knew I was going to be coming here, so I thought I'd get it for you." She handed it to him, her face reddening.

Surprised and taken aback, he took the necklace and held it up. The small links were two peculiar types of metal, almost like a sparkling copper with gray steel interweaved within the links. The true prize was the pendant. It was of a small flattened gold dove with its wings outspread. Surrounding the small bird were circular gold rings, encasing it. It wasn't a girly pendant, all pretty and dainty, but instead reminded him of a family's crest symbol. He had read about family crests in school and he thought this was really neat. "Thanks, Charity," he signed, humbled.

"Yeah, thanks, Charity," Katie said, scootching into her lap.

"Hey, Danny, put it on," Michael suggested.

Charity wrapped her arms around Katie and glanced at Danny. "Yeah, let's see it on you."

He slipped it over his head.

Charity leaned over and took out a compact from her purse and opened it up, letting him peer into the mirror. "It looks great on you." She pointed to the pendant. "You know, those circles around the dove aren't there just for show. They're called concentric circles and they're symbolic, meant as a shield to protect the bird. The craftsman told me it gives good luck and protection to those who wear it." She shrugged, looking embarrassed. "I know. I'm going to be a scientist, but here I still kind of believe in the power of charms. Very voodoo and dystopian of me. As if we're all eventually going to need charms and spells to protect ourselves one day."

He understood and thought about the dreamcatcher hanging on a peg behind his bed. He didn't think it really helped, but a guy from the FBI had given it to him a few years ago and he'd put it there, just in case it really had some sort of ability. With all the bad dreams he'd been having, it was obvious it didn't work, but he kept it just in case.

So, voodoo or not, Danny knew he could use all the luck he could get these days. "Really, I like it a lot. Thank you, Charity."

"Glad you like it." She smiled at Michael who beamed at his girlfriend.

Katie opened the book and she and Charity started slowly leafing through the pages together.

His time to talk to his sister was over.

Chapter Six

Dinner ran late and Michael was going to drive Charity to the station to catch the eight o'clock train back to New York City, but his parents suggested she stay in the guestroom for the night. She had the foresight to pack an overnight bag, just in case something came up. Ten minutes later, his brother and his girlfriend were snuggling together in the family room watching yet another movie, this time with his parents joining them. One of those R-rated ones that he wasn't allowed to see yet which had a lot of violence and bad language. They even broke out a bottle of wine and his mom made a cheese and fruit platter, like they were double dating or something. It was all he could do not to gag, but it was also probably a good thing because now he'd have a chance to talk to Katie before she went to sleep.

He found her in her room, tending to Mickey the Praying Mantis and gently stroking the creature's back. Her green flannel pajamas with smiling spider faces covered her from head to toe, with only her toes peeking out from underneath the long pants.

She turned to him, speaking and signing with one hand. "I need the flies in the jar over there on the table. Can you get them for me?" She jutted her chin towards her desk table and sure enough there were two flies buzzing around in an old pickle jar. Danny brought them to her and she released them into Mickey's aquarium, covering the screened lid quickly so they didn't escape.

It freaked Danny out to watch Mickey eat, because a mantis liked to stalk his prey. How Katie watched that thing eat them alive was crazy to him. Well, it used to seem crazy. Now his perception of things with regards to her had a whole different meaning.

They sat together quietly for a while, watching as Mickey slowly and methodically climbed over the twigs and sticks and hid himself away. It would take some time, but Danny was sure that if he walked away, the next time he came back to the cage the two buzzing flies would be toast.

Danny touched his sister's shoulder and she turned to him. "Can you understand what Mickey's thinking?"

She cocked her head and stared at the cage. "He's really happy. You can tell from the way he preens himself and how calm he is. He knows there's food in the cage."

"That's not what I mean. I mean, can you hear him? Does he speak to you?"

"Like in my head? Like with words the way you and I talk?"

Danny nodded.

Katie shook her head. "No, it's not like that. Bugs can't talk like people. They're just a whole big bunch of emotions. But, I can sense what they feel. You know, they're not just these disgusting creepy things everyone says they are. They have feelings."

"Yeah, but what about the flies you put in there? Don't they have feelings, too?"

She crinkled her nose. "Yeah, but it's a good thing they're pretty dumb. They don't even know they're going to get eaten. They're just happy they have a new place to buzz around in."

This was unbelievable. "So, Katie, what happened at the table this morning at breakfast? Why did you kill that bug instead of begging mom to let you keep it? It couldn't be because it smelled bad. Geez, a ton of bugs really stink," he signed.

Her brows furrowed in concern. "Are you going to tease me again?"

Tease her again? Did he really tease her all the time? Chagrined, he shook his head. "No, I promise."

"The bug at the table didn't feel the way other bugs felt. I've played with cockroaches before, like the ones we saw in New York City at that old apartment building." Her eyes were wide, remembering. "And Mommy kept screaming and trying to run away. That was funny. But the cockroach this morning didn't speak to me or feel the way the others did. It was as if it had only one thought in its mind, which was to find me. I know, it sounds weird, but it reminded me of the bugs I dream about."

He shook his head in understanding. A bug from a dream that was suddenly real? He, more than anyone, could empathize. "No, it isn't weird. Tell me more about it. Maybe I can help you figure out what's happening."

She thought about it and put her hand to her temple and then to the front of her head. "When I held him, my head started hurting and it smelled gross like when Mommy opened the hamburgers the other day and had to throw them out."

He remembered. "Oh, yeah, she did that because they were rotten."

Katie nodded. "That's what the bug smelled like and I knew I had to kill it or it would make everything rotten. When I smashed it to the table, my headache went away and I felt better."

He sat back, exhaling. He made a decision and took a deep breath. "You know, you just told me something I never knew about you before and now I have a secret I want to tell you. There are things I can do, too, that other people can't. We're a lot like each other, Katie." He hoped his mother wouldn't kill him for what he was about to declare. They never told Katie anything about Danny's ability with birds or his powers. His parents felt she was too little to know and that it might scare her, or worse, she might not be able to keep the secret. But, maybe they should have told her. Maybe then his parents would have realized what was going on with their own daughter, as well. He had a strong hunch they had no idea her fascination with bugs was anything more than a hobby.

Katie glanced at him sideways. "You mean how you can talk to the birds?"

His jaw dropped. "You know I can do that?"

She rolled her eyes. "Of course, I do. Every time one of your stupid birds grabs a big fat worm I have to hear it screaming in my head it knows it's going to get eaten. You sit there all smiley at your bird and happy for him that it gets to have dinner. It's horrible."

His eyes widened. "I had no idea."

She shrugged. "You look at birds the same way I look at my bugs. They're always flying near you, closer than they ever get to regular people and there's always a bunch hanging around the house, so I figured you could talk to your birds, too. I don't think Mommy and Daddy can though. I asked them once and they just laughed. Michael can't either."

He was amazed at how insightful his sister was. "But you never said anything else to them, or to me, about your bug friends? Why didn't you ask me to stop letting the birds eat the worms or something?"

She stared at him like he was crazy. "Well, it's not like the birds can eat anything else if there are no seeds around. Like these flies in Mickey's cage. I learned about this at the bug museum. Survival of the fittest. Everything has to get eaten sometime. Your birds have to eat my friends and Mickey has to eat these flies. There's not much any of us can do about it."

He remembered something weird that happened a year before and wondered if there was a connection. "Katie, do you remember when you were sick last year with the flu and all those ants and spiders invaded the house? Mom was so upset she called an emergency exterminator."

Katie nodded. "I know. I was in bed and I heard her on the phone yelling for them to come over and kill all of them. Danny, it wasn't their fault. They were just coming to see me because I was sick." She leaned towards him conspiratorially. "I made all of the bugs go away before the exterminator came."

Danny remembered how mortified his mother had been when the guy finally arrived. She had marched him into the kitchen and laundry room, and nothing was there. She'd been so frantic on the phone, demanding they show up within the hour and then, nothing. The guy probably thought she was crazy.

"How did you make them leave?"

"I just lay on my bed and sent out a message of terrible things to them. I knew they were going to die if they stayed."

"Katie, are the bugs…people?"

"People? Like you and me? No." She stared at him, squinting. "Why? Are your birds people?"

He nodded and explained how birds were vessels of the newly deceased. That they were people's souls. That when people died, their souls went into birds until they were ready to take themselves to the light. He didn't leave anything out. She listened raptly, and he realized he'd never given her enough credit. In fact, apparently no one had.

Katie shook her head. "My insects are just bugs. They're not people." They sat for a while in silence. Finally, Danny felt it was time to broach the subject again.

"Tell me about your dreams. Maybe I can help you."

She shivered. "They're really scary. There's this big mean dark tornado in them and it's trying to eat me up."

His stomach dropped. A dark tornado?

"Is it black, like a big funnel?" He used his hands to explain and she nodded.

He was suddenly chilled, and it wasn't from the temperature outside. No, this just wasn't possible. "Katie, are there bugs twisting in the tornado in your dreams, too?"

Her eyebrows widened in surprise. "How do you know? There are lots of them, but all of them are bad, like the cockroach I found in the kitchen. I told Mommy the other night about my dream when I woke up, but she told me not to worry and it was just a nightmare. I heard Mommy tell Daddy you're having bad dreams, too, and she's upset because she doesn't know what's going on with us. She thinks we're both coming down with something, but I don't feel sick. Do you?"

He shook his head and leaned towards her. "You're not going to believe this, but I'm dreaming of the bugs and the tornado, too. I don't know how, but we're dreaming the exact same thing."

Her eyes widened. "But, it's not just in my dreams. I see the tornado all the time when I'm awake. It follows me and I'm scared it's going to hurt me."

He froze. "Where do you see it?"

She bit her lip. "When I was at school the other day. I was looking out the window and it was in back of the playground, hiding behind the trees. I told the teacher, and she called Mommy because I was crying. Mommy told her I wasn't sleeping well and must be daydreaming, but I wasn't daydreaming. I saw it. Why doesn't anyone believe me?"

"I believe you." Katie's elementary school was at the other edge of town and overlooked the forest.

Katie touched his arm to make him look at her. "And the other day it was here. I was playing with Mickey and I got chilly. When I turned to the window I saw it outside, just floating there and making my window all dark. My window was open and it started to ooze into my room. I screamed and the big black bird that hangs out around the house near your window all the time flew right inside it and was squawking like crazy. Mommy and Daddy came in, but the tornado disappeared before they saw it. I think the bird got hurt, though, because he was sitting on the floor and was bleeding a little. Daddy tried to help it, but it flew out the window."

He remembered Dr. Polensky's cuts and realized he must have gotten them when he'd tried to protect his sister. He knew something about the black mass already and hadn't told him. Why not? Did he think he couldn't handle it? Or did he really not know?

His sister crept onto his lap and put her head on his chest. He patted her back. She was shivering.

The black mass was here and it wasn't just waiting at the outskirts of Magnolia Fields any longer. Here he had thought it was coming for him all along, but he had the unsettling thought that maybe it was just trying to get rid of him so it could get to Katie. Maybe she was his true target. But why? What could it possibly want with his little sister and what was the connection with the bugs? Because he believed bugs were important to it. Bugs were from the dirt.

It was at that moment he made a decision, probably one of the first adult decisions of his life. He decided there was no way he was going to let this evil ever get to his sister. He'd fight with everything he had to keep her safe.

He stared out the window trying to decide what to do next.

Then the lights went out.

Chapter Seven

He felt Katie shudder and grabbed her hand. He wouldn't be able to sign to her in the dark so with his free hand he felt against the wall to get his bearings. He was sure his mother was calling up to them, because he could feel Katie trying to move past him and go into the hallway. They reached the stairs, but he pulled her back. The hairs on the back of his neck stood up and he swore he felt like his body was being charged. Something was coming.

At that moment, the front door swung open and a gust of cold air pushed into the foyer, bringing with it a stench so vile Danny knew it could only be one thing. He felt Katie stiffen and knew she felt it, too. He pushed her backwards, dragged her into his room and slammed the door shut behind them. They huddled together on his bed and watched, horrified as a black mist seeped and oozed under his door like smoke from a fire. The temperature in the room dropped and their breath steamed in the air. He could feel the air charging and the hairs on his arms stood up.

Katie screamed and grabbed at Danny as the mass moved like an apparition into the room and formed itself into a humanoid shape. It drifted closer and closer. The smell of decay and rot permeated the air and they both gagged. The mass changed and sent out feelers. Creepy tendrils, like little legs from an octopus extended from it, snaking itself across the room and towards the bed. Bits and pieces of worms and spiders fell from the tendrils and onto the floor. The insects writhed and wiggled on the ground. Desperate, Danny glanced out the window and concentrated, sending out his energy for the birds to come help him, but nothing happened. He pushed harder and again he felt nothing. Fear seeped into his being. This had never happened before. He'd always been able to call to the birds.

He could read Katie's lips in the moonlight. "It's coming for me, Danny. It's coming to eat me. I can hear it calling to me." She clutched at him, tore his t-shirt and ripped the chain off his neck in her desperation to hold onto him. Danny grabbed the baseball bat he kept at the side of his bed and swung at the mass, but it did nothing but hit pieces of dead worms and bugs floating inside it and hurled them across the room. The mass tendrils kept advancing and he could feel their icy coldness snake by him to reach his sister. One wrapped itself around his neck and squeezed. Danny concentrated, sending out his own feelers and felt blessed energy release from him and race away to the sky. For a moment the mass shuddered and then it renewed its strength around his neck, squeezing harder as if trying to stop him.

Danny fell to the floor, grabbed his neck and tried to breathe. He glanced over and saw Katie behind him pull a trophy from his shelf and hurl it at the window. It shattered. Dr. Polensky flew through the open window, along with a throng of other birds, and together they all stormed into the mass. Danny felt their fear as if it were his own, felt their pain as the icy coldness of the mass enveloped their fragile bodies as well as his. He knew they came because of his call. Knew if they got hurt it was because of him. A moan escaped his lips as he realized the magnitude of their unselfish actions. More birds flew into the room and into the creature. The evil mass released him and began spinning and turning violently to fight the birds. He watched helplessly as they were flung out from the force, but again and again shoved themselves back in. The mass pulsated, grew bigger and then smaller and Danny could see the beast weakening. With a violent force of wind, the mass shot itself under the door and disappeared.

The lights came back on.

Danny's breath caught in his throat. His floor resembled the forest floor, covered in dirt, leaves and thousands upon thousands of bugs and worms and—dying birds.

Danny's parents pounded on the door and, with a loud crack that he actually felt in his gut. His father kicked the door in. His parents raced in and paused, shocked at the carnage. Michael and Charity were behind them, but Michael saw what was happening and held Charity back.

Danny jumped off the bed and hurried to the dying birds covering his floor. He grabbed each of them, one by one and quickly sent them off to the light. He got to Dr. Polensky last. Danny cradled him gently in his hands and rubbed Dr. Polensky's face affectionately against his back. The bird laid its broken beak tenderly on Danny's cheek.

"Be safe, Danny." Then Dr. Polensky closed his eyes. A final white light shot from Danny's hands and the bird stilled, collapsing in his hands.

Charity forced herself into the room and screamed. She turned to Michael and shoved her face into his chest.

Danny couldn't blame her. His room looked like a massacre and he was holding a dead bird in his hands, its blood running down his fingers.

Maddy stared at Danny, her face anguished. "Something's coming, isn't it?"

He nodded, not sure what else to say.

Katie pulled herself from behind Danny and signed.

"No, Mommy, it's already here."

Chapter Eight

With no possible way to clean Danny's room to make it suitable for sleeping that evening, they shut the bedroom door and bunked him with Michael for the night. Katie refused to sleep alone and curled up next to her mom in the center of her king-sized bed. The putrid smell of the mass lingered in the air and the window was open next to them.

Gary strolled into the bedroom with Danny at his side. Gary had fixed Danny's necklace and it lay snugly back around his neck. Danny wasn't letting it leave his body again. The two of them sat down on the bed as Katie and Maddy sat up. "The four of us need to talk," Gary said.

"No, the five of us need to talk." Michael came into the room.

Danny glared at him. "What, your girlfriend doesn't need you for something? She giving her lips a break?" He knew he was being obnoxious, but he didn't care. Something bad was happening and not once had he been able to talk to his brother about it. He'd been counting on him to help.

"No, her lips are just fine, but thanks for asking, Birdman." Michael turned to his parents. "I told her I needed to get some sleep. She's been up since six a.m. so she's bushed anyway and after what she saw, I'm sure she'd like to put it behind her for the night." He eyed his brother. "Look, something's going on and I want to help."

"Something certainly is," Maddy said. She turned to Danny and Katie and crossed her arms in front of her chest. "One of you better start spilling. This has been going on for a while and we're done with secrets. I've watched the two of you wake up with nightmares for weeks and come home bruised and beaten up with no explanation." She eyed Danny's neck, which had bruise marks from the mass trying to choke him. Not to mention the nicks on his cheeks from the shattered glass. "Start talking."

For a few seconds Danny and Katie stared silently at everyone and then they finally answered. Danny told them about his dreams and the black mass and about being attacked on the outskirts of Magnolia Fields. Katie told everyone she always knew about Danny's bird friends, that she could feel insects and things from the ground and that the black mass has been following her, too. His parents, and Michael, were justifiably shocked and horrified and stood there, stupefied.

"She's sort of like me, Mom. She can understand bugs, worms, and all the earth creatures. She knows how they feel," Danny said.

"I had always thought it was just a hobby. I had no idea the depth of it." Maddy took Katie's hands. "Why didn't you tell us, honey?"

"Tell you what?"

Gary shook his head. "Maddy, if this was something she could always do, she'd have no need to tell us anything. It would have been completely natural for her, just like when Danny would stare out the window at the birds when he was a baby. I mean, if we really want to think about it, she was always telling us, wasn't she? The way she'd get on the ground and play with ants as a toddler. How bees and mosquitoes never bother her or how butterflies always seem to find her."

Maddy smacked her hand to her head. "Of course. It's been in front of our eyes her whole life. And I call myself a scientist?" She turned to Gary. "How can she do this? I didn't have an accident with her and nothing out of the ordinary happened with my pregnancy except for the attack from

Herrington. Why does she have this power and what does it mean?"

"Maybe there's a genetic link? A recessive gene, which was dormant and came out in both of them?" Gary suggested. "We could run a series of gene, chromosomal, and biochemical tests on them to be sure."

Maddy nodded. "That's a good start. But what if it has something to do with me and the accident I had when I was pregnant with Danny? I could be the catalyst. Maybe the intense amount of ultraviolet rays I was hit with altered my DNA or even the RNA levels?"

Gary shook his head. "I don't think so. Danny could have been affected by the accident, but you're saying the biochemistry of your eggs was changed as well, which would have affected Katie in a similar fashion years later. How exactly?"

Maddy shook her head and shrugged.

"Hey, what about me?" Michael said. "Is there anything maybe I can do?"

Gary tilted his head. "It's possible, Michael, though I would have thought we would have seen something from you by now, don't you? Of course, if your mom's chemistry was changed and modified by the accident and it affected her eggs at that point, I don't see how. If the accident isn't what triggered all of this, then it could very well be genetic and maybe something is dormant in you as well. We'll do a series of tests on all of you to be sure." Gary turned back to Katie. "Are your bugs people, Katie? Like Danny's birds are people?"

Danny shook his head and waved the question aside. "I already asked her. They're not. She says they're just bugs. But there is something about them, something I've been thinking about that is scarier than anything that's happened so far."

"What could possibly be scarier than something evil after my children?" Maddy asked.

Danny bit his lip. It might sound crazy, but he had a hunch he was right and it scared the life out of him. "If my powers are birds and souls and heaven, and Katie's are about bugs and things from the ground, and the thing after us is cold and smells like something died, well, maybe this thing is from…" he let the sentence go unfinished.

Maddy put a hand to her mouth and trembled slightly. She realized what he was insinuating.

Gary cocked his head and spoke slowly. "Are you suggesting while you can channel things from above Katie is channeling things from the underworld?" He swallowed hard, but remained calm and turned to his daughter. "Katie, if these bugs aren't people, can you still communicate with them more than just empathically? Can you do more than just feel them?"

"Like what, Daddy?"

"Well, do they let you see things, like things that are…down below? Do they take you places, ever?"

"Take me places?"

"Yes, like in the fairytale movies you watch. Do the bugs ever take you to places that are different than here? Do the insects show you things? The reason I ask, is because birds show Danny things in the sky and take him to places with lots of light and flowers and it's peaceful and beautiful there. Do your creatures ever show you anything like that?"

Her eyes became very wide and she nodded. "They show me scary stuff, Daddy. Places like the moon and icky huge bugs with mean faces. And lots of fires. There's fire everywhere."

Maddy sucked in her breath and Gary touched her arm, shaking his head to remain calm.

Danny chimed in. "The people, Katie. Don't forget to tell them they show you people."

"What kind of people?" Michael asked, warily.

Danny told them about the creepy people in Katie's dreams. When he was done, Katie put her face to her hands and started crying. He felt bad for her. For God's sake, she was only seven. Only a year old older than he'd been when Herrington was after him. And worse, her powers took her to scary places. It was entirely different than where his birds took him.

Maddy stretched out her arms and took the little girl into them. "Ok, we're done talking about this for the night. We'll clean up Danny's room and start figuring this out tomorrow morning, okay?"

Danny clapped his hands and got his mom's attention. "Mom, I was thinking about something. Do you think the machine would work on her?"

She raised her eyebrows and considered this. "Interesting, but I don't see how, Danny. It works with electromagnetic waves."

Gary snapped his fingers. "Of course, and bugs are repelled by those very waves. Brilliant idea, Danny. There is a direct connection to bugs and waves, Maddy. We should have thought of this sooner. And, if this is indeed a genetic trait, or your biochemistry was altered in some way where both kids are susceptible, the kids might have some sort of sensitivity to the waves discernible only to them."

"You mean like how a pest repeller works when you put the frequency on high and the bugs leave an area, but it doesn't affect anyone else?" Michael asked. "You know Charity would know the most about this. It is her line of study. We should talk to her about it."

Gary shook his head. "Absolutely not. I don't want to involve her."

"But, Dad—"

Gary shook his head, his voice firm. "Look, it's for the same reason your mother and I decided Danny's gifts weren't to be shared with the world. If Katie has a similar gift, we must find out the depths of it first before we decide who to share this knowledge with. I don't know Charity well, and as nice and lovely as she is, and despite the fact that she's your girlfriend, she's not family."

Michael's jaw dropped and his eyes widened indignantly. "What do you think she's going to do? You think she's some evil scientist ready to swoop in and claim the gift that will bring us all to the depths of hell? Why don't you have the FBI come in and arrest her before we find out she's really a bug in disguise, or this black mass herself?"

Maddy squinted at him. "Michael, please do us all a favor and leave the melodramatics out of this. You know what we mean. Your father is right. The fewer people who know, the better, and if we need to ask Charity specific questions on the field, we'll bring her in, okay? But before we do anything, I'd like to try to work with Katie on the machine tomorrow, just for a test run. But I don't want everyone to get their hopes up. Michael, remember when we tried it on you a few years back and you got so upset when nothing happened and all the lights all stayed off? It most likely won't work on her either, as it's been calibrated to Danny's abilities."

Gary nodded. "Not to mention birds and insects respond on entirely different frequency levels as well, so it may not work for that reason. And for that matter, Maddy, it could be the kids' own abilities respond differently, too. I mean, we don't even really understand what it is Katie's channeling and feeling in the first place, or what will happen even if she does get the lights on."

"And if she does get them on," Maddy said, "will it take her somewhere and if so, where? And then the next question is who or what would she bring here? Will it be the bugs and creatures she plays with or something else entirely?"

Danny piped in. "Yeah, and take it one step further, will she go up, like I do, or…somewhere else?"

Gary nodded. "We'll start her slowly and monitor her the entire time so it doesn't get out of control if it actually works."

And with that, Danny and Michael went back to Michael's room and Katie fell asleep in the middle of both her parents.

No one had the chance to dream.

Late that same evening, a fastidious man lay on his cot situated in the far left hand corner of his six-by-ten prison cell. His thin, light blue blanket and sheets were folded into perfect military preciseness. The walls were a white painted cinderblock with not a single poster or drawing on them to make the room more homey. The inmate didn't want that. Beyond a small bookshelf, a lidless steel toilet and a sink attached to the wall were the only things to break the starkness. The shelf was also steel and attached to the wall. There were no bolts or nails to be seen. Nothing to mar the surface or underside or that could be used as a potential weapon. On the shelf were three things. One was an eight-by-ten wedding picture of the man holding onto the arm of a striking blond woman. She was regally beautiful, with the air of a queen. Her hair was pulled back from her face in a severe bun, and an ornate diamond tiara rested atop her head. An intricately laced veil was fastened to it and the beaded, pearl festooned train of the veil ran down her slender back. The woman's eyes were an unusual icy-blue color. She appeared aloof and stared unsmilingly at the camera, her eyes menacing, as if she were angry at the photographer. In fact, he remembered, she had been. She had told the photographer no more photos, but he had snapped this one anyway and had paid for it dearly. The prisoner loved this photo more than anything, though. It showed his beloved at her very best. The photograph was now curling at the edges as the prison guards would not allow him to have a picture frame to keep it safe.

The second thing appeared to be nothing more than a small, exceedingly light tin of round green mints from the commissary, and had the prison guards thought it was any different, it would have been confiscated long ago. The prisoner was obsessed with his breath, among so many other compulsive traits that seemed to threaten his sanity. The visiting prison psychologist assured the warden that allowing the man to calm this one obsessive peculiarity, over all his other obsessive-compulsive tendencies, would allow him to be a more compliant prisoner. And he was, but not for the reason they thought. Each perfectly lined-up candy was actually a key on a phone, a small receiver peeking out the back where one would think was simply a clasp. Where the barcode appeared was the microphone, the ingredients label, the speaker.

The man waited the requisite three hours after lights-out by quietly humming Wagner. He then slowly sat up. The penitentiary had gone to sleep for the night. He could hear the snoring from the inmate next door and the tinny sounds of the television the guard at the end of the hall played constantly. He listened further—to the sounds of the water dripping outside his window from the rainstorm earlier in the day, to the quick tap-tap-taps of the feet of the guard who had just moved past his cell to make yet another circuit around this particular cell block. He would return in thirty-five minutes. It was enough time for him to do what needed to be done.

The man rested his hands on his thighs and stood, his knees cracking from remaining still for so long. Gone were his jeweled rings and perfectly tailored suits, replaced with the orange prison jumper he'd worn for the past seven years since he'd been captured after kidnapping Maddy and Gary

Anderson and trying to gain control of their sons. Seven-plus years since his beloved wife had died, in a hospital far away from him while he had screamed in anguish from his prison cell. The travesty was that after everything he had done, he couldn't even be at her side when she moved on. It preyed on his mind day in and day out.

His graying hair, normally worn long and slicked back, was cut close to his skull so he could tame his unruly curls. He moved the three steps to the tin, bypassing the photo, and picked up the phone. Opening the lid, he dialed the number, then put the phone to his ear, after placing his pillow over his mouth to muffle the sound.

The connection went through and was picked up on the first ring. He heard crickets in the background. "Are you there?"

"Yes."

"Is it working?"

"Of course it is, and brilliantly I might add. I made some additional modifications to the calibrations myself this past week for added efficiencies."

"Excellent." He paused. "I don't have to tell you I need the girl undamaged."

"Of course, you don't. I already know that."

"It's not going to be easy," Herrington said. "You're going to have to eventually get rid of the boy to get to her."

"I know, but not just yet. I need him. He's helping me to move her along faster."

"Soon you won't need him at all and the quicker you rid yourself of him, the better."

"I understand, but it's going to be hard. He's being protected by the birds and they're very strong. Much stronger than we thought."

Samuel Herrington sucked in his breath and counted to fifteen. Enough time to calm himself.

The caller waited.

"I don't care if it's hard. Do what you have to do. I need the girl or everything is for naught."

"You'll have her, but I need more time with her."

"We don't have more time. I want her now. Move her along faster." And with that, he ended the call.

Samuel Herrington put the pack of mints back on his bookcase and gently touched the face of the woman in the photo with his index finger. It left a small sheen of oil on the surface and he used his sleeve to gently wipe it off. The man wanted this woman back in his life so badly for a moment he nearly lost his composure. His finger shook and he turned, glancing at the third object on his bookshelf. A dead, dried, black fifteen-millimeter-long scorpion sat there, glued to the bookshelf so he could never use it for anything other than decoration. Another suggestion from the psychologist. Herrington stared at the creature's body and its beautifully segmented tail with its perfect stinger. He started to feel overwhelmed and felt a great need to start counting, to wash his hands, to tap his feet. Instead, he brought his finger to the stinger and pushed hard. The stinger pierced his skin and while the venom had long since dried up and gone, the pain was enough to allow him to focus.

He stared at the drop of blood on his finger and put it to his lips. "Soon, Marta," he whispered. "I promised I would come get you."

With that, he lay back down on his cot, counted backwards from a hundred to one in English, German, and French, and then fell into a dreamless sleep.

A lone person stood in the backyard of the Andersons' house and closed the cell phone. An army of spiders, ants and beetles huddled around the stranger's feet. Herrington's assistant took a small device from a pocket and pressed a button. A sharp, keening noise pierced the night and a small wind picked up, scattering leaves around them. With a further turn of the dial, the noise finally disappeared. Only then did the bugs disperse, shoving themselves deep into unseen crevices in the earth, disturbed by the sound and seeking a way to escape from it.

The worker stared back at the house, at the shattered window in Danny's bedroom and then turned to the parents' bedroom. The lights were off. Michael's room was dark, too, now that he and Danny had finally gone back to sleep. Then the worker's eyes traveled down to the first floor guest bedroom. A small nightlight flickered through the window curtains, which were swaying slightly from the wind moving through the open window. Yes, that was where to start.

The worker took out another device and pressed a button sending electromagnetic waves into the air. The sound of crackling, resembling electric charges, popped around them and lights began springing from the unit. Perfect.

The worker walked towards the house and towards the guest bedroom window.

Now it would truly begin.

Chapter Nine

Charity was screaming so loudly they could hear her all the way upstairs.

Michael jumped out of bed so fast Danny tumbled to the floor in a heap of blankets. Together they raced down the steps and burst into the guest room. Danny was shocked at the sight of Charity racing around the room batting at herself frantically while covered in honey bees. There were hundreds buzzing throughout the room. They were darting in and out of the open window and attaching themselves to her nightshirt, her hair, and her bare legs.

She jumped up and down and flailed at the insects, trying to shake them off her face. Her head was a massive whirl of curls. "Michael, get them off of me! Get them off of me!"

Michael grabbed a pillowcase and swatted at them, but the bees simply jumped from Charity and attacked him.

Maddy and Gary rushed into the room, Katie at their side. Danny turned to his sister and signed quickly. "Can you do anything?"

She stared at him, her mouth open. "Me? What can I do?"

"Danny, get Katie out of here. Both of you, and shut the door behind you." Gary signed, pushing his daughter back, and then tried to help Charity.

Instead of leaving, Danny grabbed Katie and dragged her over to the corner of the room by the closet. He swatted a bee off his cheek. His breath came fast. "Close your eyes and feel for them. See if you can reach them and tell them to leave." A bee rested itself on his wrist and he flicked it away. It hadn't gone unnoticed to him that not one of them was touching his sister. His hunch might work.

Katie stared around the room and shook her head, confused. "They're scared. They don't know what they're doing. Something's making them do this." Her eyes bubbled with tears.

Danny grabbed her hands as a bee stung his neck and he flinched in pain. God, that hurt. "Just try," he signed. "Talk to them and send them away. Like you told them to leave when mommy called the exterminator. They like you, see? None of them are touching you. Tell them if they stay they're going to die." Another bee rested on his shirt and another settled on his shoulder. "Fast, Katie, or I'm going to get stung again." He felt one pierce his arm and smacked it hard.

She turned to the bees and became very still. For a second, the noise in the room intensified, and the buzzing increased, because he felt the vibration in his chest, when suddenly Danny sensed a small charge whisk by him. Then, as one, the bees took flight and soared out through the open window. With a cry, Charity collapsed into Michael's arms and Gary ran over and shut the window.

They stood there stunned, all of them covered with bee stings. All, except Katie.

Danny turned to her. "Are they gone?"

She nodded. "For now, but I don't think they'll be gone for long."

After painstakingly picking out twenty-one stingers from her body, they ended up taking Charity to the emergency room just to make sure she didn't have any allergies or bad reactions. It was a good thing. It turned out she wasn't allergic to them, but she swelled up from the sheer amount of stings. She didn't have any family in New York, so Maddy insisted she stay with them until she felt better and the swelling and itching went down. When Charity refused her offer, Maddy would hear none of it.

"Charity, don't be ridiculous," Maddy said at breakfast the next morning, her own cheeks swollen from stings she suffered. "I feel just horrible about this, and we've got plenty of room. Don't forget, both Gary and I are doctors."

Danny rolled his eyes. "You're scientists, not doctors, Mom." He scratched at the bite on his neck, which itched liked crazy.

Gary looked indignant. "We may not be Emergency Room trauma surgeons, but we know enough to treat bee stings, young man." He turned back to Charity. "Really, Charity, it's absolutely no problem and it's the least we can do. And Danny, stop scratching. You'll open it up and give yourself an infection."

Charity stared at Michael, and tried to speak through her swollen lips. "You donth mand if I thtay a wittle wonger?" She put her head down and covered her face with her gauze-wrapped hands.

Michael bent to her, removed her hands and cupped her chin with his own bandaged hand until she looked up at him.

"No, I donth mand," he joked back.

It was enough. She smacked him on the arm, after grimacing a bit, and agreed to stay until the swelling went away.

Maddy gave Charity some Benadryl, lathered her up with calamine lotion and had her lie down in the guest bedroom with a bunch of icepacks. Michael stayed by her side until she fell asleep.

Maddy called to Katie as she skipped into the kitchen. "Ok, now that Charity's asleep, let's give this a try, shall we? Danny, come along and help me." The three of them went to the finished basement and settled themselves on the plush carpet. Katie plopped herself on a beanbag and watched

Maddy unlock the wall safe in the corner of the room. Reaching inside, she brought out a big black box with light bulbs and dials on it.

"What is that?" Katie asked, craning her head to look.

Maddy placed it on the carpeted floor. "Daddy and I built this device when Danny was a baby. We all call it The Machine. When your brother was a little boy and told us he could talk to birds, your daddy and I made this unit to help heighten his abilities. It has the capability to use electromagnetic waves." She sat on the floor and took her daughter's hands and then ran her fingers up and down Katie's arms until she started laughing. "Feel that?"

"It tickles," Katie said, giggling.

"It should," Maddy said. "You see, honey, every living cell in every living being on this planet has something called an electromagnetic field within them. Electric currents run through every single one of your muscles and nerves and the currents start working once you begin doing things like walking around or running, tickling each other or even flapping our hands." Maddy pumped her daughter's hands up and down to show her an example. "See? We're creating energy just by doing this. Do you understand?"

"A little, I think," Katie giggled.

Danny was quite sure she didn't understand. It was hard having scientists for parents and while Danny appreciated that they talked to him like an adult, sometimes it was hard to follow their conversations. His parents always forgot they were just kids.

He tried to help. "It means there is power everywhere, Katie. And it's not just people who have that kind of power. Animals have it and so do my birds and your insects."

Maddy nodded. "That's right. All animals, bugs, and humans have it, but birds really seem to take it one step further than the rest of us. Birds can use the earth's magnetic fields to help them navigate and travel over long distances, like when they migrate from New York all the way to Florida in the wintertime. People always wonder how is it they know where to go."

Danny nodded. "It's not like they have a map they can take with them when they want to go to Disneyworld, right?"

His mother turned and adjusted a few dials on the machine. "We believe birds use the magnetic fields to interact with their own electric currents and it puts them in the right direction. It's fascinating."

"Tell her about the blue light with the birds, Mom," Danny signed.

Maddy turned to her daughter and grinned, clasping her hands on her knees. "Well, this is going to sound very magical, but some people believe there's this special molecule in a bird's eye and it can react to changing magnetic fields. That when it becomes sensitive to magnetic fields it changes from a blue light that goes into their eye from the spectrum, and gets lighter or darker at times reacting to the fields, so they can figure out which way to travel."

Katie crinkled her nose, clearly confused so Danny jumped in again. "I'll give you an example. You know that cool mood ring you have upstairs that Michael got you? Depending on how you feel, the temperature of your body changes the color in the ring. For birds, it's like a mood ring in their eyes. Scientists believe this blue light changes when the birds become sensitive to different magnetic fields of the earth when they're flying. So, basically, if the color changes one way, they go in one direction, if it changes to a different color or shade, they change their course."

"I couldn't have explained it better myself," Maddy beamed. "Your dad and I do get a little longwinded in our explanations and forget who we're talking to." Maddy turned back to the machine and then put her notebook next to it and flipped through the pages. She found a blank page, dated it and turned back to Katie. "Now, your brother can react to certain energy fields and I'd like to see if you're able to react to any of the energy forces as well. Let's have some fun and give it a try, okay? Just don't be upset if it doesn't work. It didn't work on Michael and he had such a fit. We'll just go very slowly and see what happens."

Maddy placed her hands on the unit and glanced at Danny with a grin. "For old time's sake, do you want to turn it on?"

Danny nodded and then paused. "But, wait a second. I don't want Katie ripping anything off of me if something goes wrong and she gets scared again." He removed a leather friendship bracelet his friend Laura from school had made him, another one around his ankle and then removed the chain pendant Charity had given him. He laid all of them gently on the table against the wall where they'd be safe. Then, without even turning towards the machine, Danny flicked on the first dial and the corresponding light bulb lit up.

Katie squealed with delight and clapped her hands. "It's magic! Do more."

"Show off." His mom placed a headset on Katie. "This will help you concentrate, honey. You'll be able to hear me, but it will get rid of the background noise and if you can feel anything, it will just be vibrations. Now, I want you to close your eyes and for starters, I just want you to sit and relax. See if you can feel any energy with the first light on. See if there is any tingling on your skin or if you can feel anything other than just the air circulating around you."

Katie sat cross-legged on the floor. She closed her eyes, but couldn't help peeking now and then to see if her mom and Danny watched.

"Close your eyes, honey. I promise I'm not going anywhere." Maddy toyed with the machine dials, increasing and decreasing the frequencies on the electromagnetic spectrum until she saw the needles find a comfortable frequency level.

His mom had initially built this machine when he was a baby, combining her research on light therapy and electromagnetic waves to create a unit that worked with all forms of waves, including telepathic mind waves.

Danny knew his parents had always found telepathy an interesting concept and combined this concept with him when they were learning about his abilities. They believed telepathy couldn't be explained away as a hoax, and they also believed there was a link between telepathy and electromagnetic waves. They were so sure mind waves played a role in electromagnetism, they had modified this machine to work with the extremely low energies of both concepts and tried to figure out the link for Danny to use his own mind stream waves to control it. The concept was to combine his own mind stream waves with electromagnetic waves and heighten his awareness of whatever power he actually had.

Maddy stared back at Katie, but she just sat there, still peeking.

Danny pushed a little in his head and popped the second light on. His mother arched her eyebrows and shook her head for him to stop there.

Katie sucked in her breath. "I hear something." She put her hand to her temple and squinted. "And my head hurts a little."

Maddy frowned. "Don't go any higher, Danny." She grabbed the notebook and started scribbling furiously. "Katie, what do you hear?"

Katie's eyes widened. "I think I hear people crying."

Danny concentrated as well. He, of course, couldn't hear anything, and at a level two he could see shimmers in the air, but nothing more. Katie turned her head whippet fast and glanced behind her. Sure enough, Danny saw a shadow dart behind the chair and plummet into the floor vent. A chill went through him. It definitely wasn't one of his birds. Katie was channeling something else entirely.

The third light went on. And then the fourth.

"Danny, stop it!" his mother ordered. "I told you not to go any higher yet."

He put up his hands defensively. "I didn't do it, Mom."

Shadows bolted around the room. They weren't little wisps of bird shadows with light feathers tickling his skin as they whisked past him. These little licks burned his cheeks and pinched him. He turned towards the dials and tried to shut them off, while his mother manually tried to turn them down, but they didn't move. In fact, the fifth light came on.

There was a small window on ground level outside and Danny could see birds bashing themselves into it to try to get in. The light was calling to them, but not in a good way. He could feel it in his very bones. He called out to them to stop and tried to send them away, but Katie's cry stopped him.

He turned to his sister and gasped. Shadowy mutated creatures flew around her. She held onto her forehead with both hands as if she had a headache and then the sixth light went on. At that moment in the corner of the room, black smoke oozed from the floor vent. Katie began to scream.

The mass was coming. Danny ran to his sister and grabbed onto her.

Maddy stood up, stared at the corner where Katie and Danny looked and then back at her kids. "What do you both see? Tell me, what is it? And what's that horrible smell?"

"It's the black mass, Mom," Danny signed. "It's coming though the floor vent right now."

His mother yelled at him. "Turn it off now. Get to level fifteen as fast as you can and turn it off." She turned to her daughter who was crying and trying to crawl backwards away from the mass.

But Danny couldn't move. He was frozen. The mass was now forming into a large shape. A tendril started to push out from it, like a wispy thread, searching for them. Dread filled his stomach. With a determination he didn't know he had, he let go of Katie, turned back to the machine and concentrated on the lights so hard his nose bled. He ignored it and forced the dials to shut down. He held out his hand and stretched. He pushed with all his might. His fingers began to tingle and the sixth light on the machine flickered. He could feel something fighting him. Something was determined to keep that light on. More birds slammed into the window and one of them broke the glass and fell into the room in a bloody mess. Glass shards scattered across the floor.

Maddy threw herself onto her daughter and cradled her. Danny turned to the mass, which had reared up higher and started to extend more of its tendrils, and with all his strength, he shut off the sixth light. He grunted as something sharp kicked him in his shins, but he ignored it, concentrating only on the lights. Something poked his cheeks, as sharp as needles. He ignored them and forced the fifth light off. Piercing burns popped up and down his arms, but again, he drowned out the pain. He wasn't going to let it win; wasn't going to let it stop him. He pushed his mind hard and the fourth and third light fizzed out.

It was enough. The black mass receded back into the vent like a disappearing puff of smoke and the control weakened. With a shuddery breath, he shut off the second light.

Maddy reached over and yanked at the last dial, slamming it off.

Katie threw the headset to the ground and shoved herself deep into her mother's arms.

Maddy held her daughter and rocked her. "No morc, Katie. I promise. We won't do this ever again."

But Danny knew just because his mother decided they wouldn't use the machine again, this wasn't the end. Now that something was happening, he knew they couldn't wait any longer. They had to find out what Katie was conjuring. "Mom, tell me you saw the black apparition in the corner of the room this time? Did you see the shadows forming with each new light bulb?"

Maddy bit her lip. "I didn't see anything. I never have. I did smell something like rotten meat. The same smell from your room the other night, but I don't have the ability to see anything except the beings in this physical realm." She stared at the dead bird on the floor, the broken glass and then turned to her son. Her forehead crinkled in concern. "Danny, you're hurt. Your face and arms are covered in welts and your nose is bleeding." She turned to Katie and saw red marks on her arms appearing as well. "What happened? Oh my God, what did they do to you both?"

Danny wiped his nose on his sleeve and moved over to his sister. "They attacked us when we tried to fight them. Katie, tell Mom what happened," he signed. "Tell her what you felt. Can you do that?"

She sniffled and nodded. "I saw bad things, Mommy. Things from the ground that wanted to come up and hurt us. They were calling to me, trying to take me somewhere so they could eat me. And they hurt my head."

Maddy stared at Danny, dumbstruck. "I don't understand. It wasn't your birds that came? I saw them at the window."

"No, Mom. My birds were never there. This is something entirely different. Not stuff that can fly up, but stuff that lives down below."

"But the birds were trying to get to you. Just like when we were training, the birds would try to reach the light when we worked on the machine."

"It's different. Those birds back then were trying to get to the light, but the good kind. The light that sends them up to level fifteen. The birds today were drawn to whatever bad energy this black mass is putting out. They don't understand it, but they have some sort of connection to it and can't help but respond."

"Then why did you keep turning on the lights, Danny? Why did you make all these things come forward if you knew it was bringing something bad?"

"I didn't turn on the other lights. Katie did."

Maddy stared at her daughter, swallowed hard and tried to keep herself calm. "You turned them on, Sweetie? All of them? All by yourself? How did you do that?"

The little girl shrugged. "I don't know. My head started hurting and when I looked at the machine, I saw things. They looked like ripply rainbows, but they were only gray and black and white. I tried to touch them and when I did the lights flicked on. Every time a light came on my headache went away for a little bit, but then all these horrible things came each time."

Maddy bit her lip. "The waves you're reacting to are definitely different than your brother's." She leaned over and quickly grabbed a small handheld electronic device. Turning the unit on, she stood and moved slowly around the room, holding the gadget in her hands.

"What are you checking for?" Danny asked at the same time that his father came bolting down the stairs.

"I'm measuring the photons charged. This is so unusual. Normally this unit would emit only low-energy frequencies."

Gary tried to interrupt. "What happened? A ton of birds just flew right into the house and then I heard glass shattering." He stared at the basement window as Katie jumped into his lap. He glanced at her and then at Danny in disbelief. "What happened down here? And that smell? It smells like what came to the house the other night. The black mass was here again?"

Maddy nodded. "The kids say it was."

Gary touched Danny's face. "Are you okay? Your nose is bleeding."

Danny tried to smile. "I'm okay now, Dad."

He stared at his daughter, noticing the welts on her arms. "Did the machine work on her?"

Maddy nodded again. "She turned on the sixth light, Gary. The sixth! I would never have believed it, and when she turned each one on, instead of bringing birds and feelings of euphoria, it had a negative reaction. It gives her headaches and brings… other things." She pursed her lips, still measuring her readings.

Gary stared at Katie and leaned his face close to hers. "Other things that hurt you?" He glanced at Danny, his eyes wide. "Hurt both of you?"

Danny nodded. "I'm telling you. She's channeling things from below."

"What came? What exactly did she conjure up?" Gary asked.

"The tornado from our dreams, Dad," Danny signed. "It came through the floor vent and into the room, just like it came into the house the other night. That's why it smells so bad. This thing is made up of dead things."

Maddy's gaze was fixated on the electromagnetic unit she was holding. She shook her head disbelievingly. "The unit's beeping," she said.

"What's it reading?" Gary tried to peer over Katie's shoulder.

Maddy sucked in her breath. "It shouldn't be reading anything more than a simple radio wave, and at the most I would have expected ultraviolet waves. But for a brief second, it recorded the intensity of a gamma ray. That isn't possible."

"A gamma ray?" Danny asked. "Isn't that radiation or something? Isn't that like when there's an explosion in space?"

"I'm not reading one that high, but it's high enough for me to be worried," Maddy said. "Normal exposure to gamma radiation is 25 mrem at most, but I'm seeing readings of close to 7,000. If it were over 10,000 I'd be absolutely horrified."

Gary spoke quickly. "Even though it's at 7,000 we have to get the dosimeters and check their radiation levels immediately to be sure."

She nodded. "I'll get them from the lab." She stood.

"Don't forget the iodide pills, too, just to be on the safe side. And please, be careful, the roads are icy."

"I will." She turned to Katie. "And don't worry, we're not going to work with this machine on you ever again, you understand me? I'm serious, Katie." And with that, she boxed it up and locked it in the safe in the closet. Then she ran upstairs to drive to the lab.

But as Danny watched his father bring Katie upstairs to treat her wounds and calm her down over a bowl of ice cream, he knew it wasn't going to be so simple. He knew that once you realized what you were doing, you didn't ever need the machine to get to the upper levels of your ability. He could call the birds to him and travel to level fifteen whenever he wished. And Katie was apparently already on level six. He wondered how much higher she could have gone if he hadn't stopped her? It gave him shivers to think about it. Her powers and capabilities seemed to be stronger and more powerful than his. What if one day he couldn't stop her? What if she already didn't even need the machine?

And as scary as that thought was, the worst part was her "gifts" didn't bring birds and happy places. It didn't bring a sense of peace and calm. It brought bad things. Things that hurt.

As Danny followed his dad, one question still lingered in his mind over all others. What if the beings from below ended up being more powerful than those from above? How was he ever going to be able to fight against them? He wiped his bloody nose on his sleeve and rubbed at the welts on his arm and with a grimace, followed the rest of his family upstairs.

Chapter Ten

Danny's dream that night was different than the others before it. Usually he was alone in his imaginings as the main character, and he'd come upon people needing help from whatever catastrophe was coming their way. Tonight Katie was there with him.

They lounged on the grass on a small hill in Magnolia Fields. Katie played with the wildflowers that were scattered across the meadow and he rested his back against a tree. Everything was vivid to him in this dream—from the way the wispy lilac-colored wildflowers bent to her touch when Katie reached out her little hand, to the smell of the wild rose bushes that bordered the park. A cool breeze blew his hair across his forehead, and when he looked to the sky, it was a startling blue and filled with white, puffy clouds. A huge yellow sun glared down on him, so bright it hurt his eyes and he had to squint. The pain felt so real and the heat of the sun on his arms was so strong he wondered if he would get a sunburn from it.

A group of blue jays flew down next to Katie. They pecked at the ground feverishly, then turned towards the sun and flapped their wings as if they were going to fly away when suddenly they settled down again. Danny could tell they were agitated and tried to talk to them, but they completely ignored him. They concentrated only on his sister. He sent out a push to them, but they disregarded his advances. Katie turned to them and held out her hands and Danny was surprised to see them filled with wriggling earthworms as if her fingers were actually Medusa's hair filled with snakes. Without a second's hesitation, the birds began attacking his sister, pecking at the food in her hands and jabbing into her skin. He yelled at her to move, but she just stood there crying and remained immobile as if she were rooted to the spot. He leaped over to help her and tried to bat the birds away, but they took flight again. The birds rose above them and then in a furious burst of violence, they descended on Katie and ripped their talons into her arms viciously.

He threw himself onto his sister, seeing but not hearing her screams with each jab and pierce, but she didn't move while the blood ran down her forearms and pooled on the ground beside her. Danny grabbed the birds and threw them aside. They lay writhing on the ground and convulsed as if the worms they had eaten had been poisonous.

Helpless, the beings rose out of their bird bodies and shrieked in agony. Their faces distorted and grew longer until they appeared as grim reapers, with their skulls shining through their skin. Danny tried to save them, to reach into them and send their souls to the light above, but instead of moving up, the beings plummeted to the ground, disappearing into the earth. He could imagine their shrieks in his mind like a big red scream.

Danny woke with a start and sat up in bed, shaking. Michael turned over and yawned. "Hey, you okay? What's the matter? You have another bad dream?" Danny was rooming with his brother even though he was still miffed at him. While they had cleaned his room, Danny didn't want to admit he was too scared to sleep by himself. He thought if Michael were there, maybe the black mass would leave him alone. Now he realized he couldn't escape it no matter where he was. It could just seek him out while he was sleeping.

The door opened and Danny and Michael glanced over.

Katie stood in the doorway and then held out her arms. "I'm bleeding."

Michael bolted out of bed. "What happened to you?" He grabbed his sister and turned on the lights. Her palms and forearms were riddled with bloody cuts. "You look like you've been slashed with a knife! Who did this to you?"

Danny stared at her, horrified and she looked back at him accusingly.

Their parents joined them and Maddy bent down to Katie, holding out her arms. "What happened to you? Who did this?"

"Danny's birds did this. I had a nightmare and these mean birds attacked me." She turned to Danny. "I gave them some food and they hurt me."

Danny swallowed hard and watched his mother grab one of Michael's t-shirts and wrap it around her daughter's arms. "The cuts are superficial, thank God," she said.

"Danny just had a nightmare, too," Michael said. He turned to his brother. "Were there birds in your dream, too, Danny? Did they attack Katie in your dream, as well?"

Danny nodded. His dream birds had assaulted his sister, in the very same dream. She had become physically hurt from it in this reality. How was that even possible?

"Ouch. That hurts." Katie said, squinting and rubbing her forehead.

Danny felt a charge in the air and glanced around frantically. Was it starting again? Oh God, what was coming? "Something's here right now!"

Katie's eyes cleared and she put down her hands. "Whew, it's better now. That was a strong one, though."

Danny gulped back bile as the charge dissipated.

Katie said it was better. But for how long?

Out in the Andersons' backyard a lone person watched the light in Michael's room turn on and shadows dart about as people moved around the room feverishly. The stranger adjusted the dials on the black box, one similar to Maddy

Anderson's except this one was equipped with frequencies and specialized adaptations that controlled other things. Things Danny didn't even know about or have any power over. Samuel Herrington had designed this unit himself years ago.

The eighth light was lit and the ninth light came on for a brief second. A blackness swelled from the earth and moved towards the house, but before it got further, the person quickly shut the unit off. "Excellent." Katie had just moved up to level nine all on her own, right in front of her family. "Not yet, little one. We'll do this at my pace, not yours." Herrington's assistant flicked down the other dials as well.

Three dead blue jays lay on the ground. With a press of a button on a small handheld device, hoards of insects began oozing out of the earth and soon covered the dead birds. They would feast on their carcasses all night. With their souls already shattered, the evidence of them would be gone by morning. Used and discarded.

The assistant hid the machine within a copse of trees in the backyard and opened a notebook, checking off a line on a long spreadsheet filled with numbers and figures.

It was all moving according to plan. And the best part? The machine worked beautifully. With Katie's sensitivity to insects, Herrington figured correctly she would have an ability to hear ultrasonic sounds most humans couldn't hear, or how else could she communicate with them? Danny's birds could only hear in the lower kilohertz range, so they wouldn't even be able to help until the very air became charged and then it would be too late for them to do anything. The birds would already be under their control.

All that had to be done to get Katie's lessons started was set the device at a higher reading, which was even higher than a dog's upper frequency level. Weekly visits to the house over the past few months had been necessary to get the machine integrated into Katie's daily life, but just two weeks ago the sound frequencies were introduced, and they had worked perfectly. Standing outside her classroom, watching through the window, the worker turned it on, and immediately Katie's head perked up. She could sense it, and she'd rub her head in pain as the frequency was slowly increased. And no one could understand what she was yammering about as she pointed to her ears and out the window, apparently trying to tell someone she heard something. Of course, no one believed her because none of them could hear anything in the first place. Apparently Maddy Anderson blamed the entire episode, and her daughter's subsequent nightmares, on Katie just not sleeping well. The little girl couldn't possibly sleep well when a machine was working on her.

So now, when experimenting and changing the sound frequencies, Katie's headache would automatically start. Now that her body was acclimated, it would self-seek a way to soothe her pain. Innately, her body learned to attack the sound and the very electromagnetic energy in the air would change and begin to charge. It was the same reaction as if they had turned on the dials for her themselves. All the little girl knew was as soon as her body pushed through a charge, it attacked her pain and her headache left. So the experiment was tested repeatedly, until it was so natural for Katie to push the waves, it became as easy for her as breathing. Doing it while she and Danny slept was the perfect idea. By conducting the experiments while they were asleep, both children could be reached at the same time and it sped up Katie's learning time exponentially. Without him even knowing it, Danny was helping her along. The machine also worked on Danny and when they both dreamed he and Katie's mind waves synced to the same currents and telepathically they were linked. And the craziest part was Maddy had been working on the telepathic path angle all along. Stupid woman, she never could figure out how to hide her lab notes better. It had been so easy to find out what she was doing and integrate it into the present agenda.

Now her children would pay dearly again. Maddy and Gary were spending their time reading about photon levels and playing with theories, while their daughter's powers were building up daily. Katie was now capable of powering the machine by herself and making herself stronger day by day. All the worker had to do was push her. Make the headaches come, adjust the electromagnetic frequencies on the machine and let Katie do the rest, pressing her a little bit further each time. There had been the slight chance she would fight it or wouldn't be as strong as she was, but that had fortunately not been the problem. The child was talented and was moving up the dials fast. All that was needed was a little more time.

"How high must she be before the event will work?" Herrington's assistant asked.

"She must be at least level fourteen," Herrington said. "At that point her powers will be mature enough to move the last dial quickly. It will be like what happened with Danny at the lab. But Katie is stronger, as we know."

The assistant let out the smallest of sighs. "Yes, I do know. I've been monitoring her for years."

"Don't get an attitude with me. I know you have. I'm not stupid," Herrington admonished. "It was a stroke of luck for us that Maddy Anderson was already pregnant. Had I known, I would have gotten rid of Gary immediately and kept her imprisoned in the labs."

"You're lucky the child wasn't injured by your men's inquisition of her mother. Luckier that the child possessed an ability at all."

The disgust in Herrington's voice was apparent. "None of this was luck. I plan for every contingency."

"Except for the fact that the Andersons were traitors. You gave them everything they ever wanted and they were spying on you behind your back the entire time. But that is not the problem now. The problem is Danny. He feels all of the charges we're manipulating. He knows something's happening."

"True, but he doesn't understand what it is and if you do your job right, he never will. He's just a kid and a deaf one at that. He won't be able to hear the sound frequencies and doing it while he's dreaming will give us the excuse he's simply having a nightmare. The birds won't be able to tell him a thing since the machine confuses them. We'll keep him in the dark for as long as possible and simply get rid of him once he's of no more use to us. Use him for the dreams to get Katie stronger and then dispose of him like we planned."

"He could cause us trouble in the meantime," the assistant said. "His birds are linked to the same frequency as the black mass. They already respond when he calls to them for help, and they weaken the mass when they attack it."

"Why do you persist in calling it the black mass?" Herrington snarled. "There is nothing black about it. It is life, energy, and vibrancy. It is absolute power."

"I call it the black mass because that's how Danny refers to it, along with calling it the tornado and a host of other names. It's best we use the same terms."

Herrington sighed. "Fine, call it what you will." He paused for a moment, apparently thinking. "So back to the machine. Some of the birds are confused by the machine and others can withstand it? Interesting. They must be the stronger ones, possibly those who are not newly deceased. I want you to create some sort of damper for the boy, and by the time he realizes what's going on, if he ever does, it will be too late for him to do anything."

"He's a smart kid," the assistant said.

Herrington scoffed. "What does that matter? His parents have never given him enough credit. They should have been discussing their theories with him for years, brought his powers to the forefront of science and into the public realm, but no. They've chosen to hide them away for their own selfish purposes. Imbeciles. They are the antithesis of what true scientists are and they are woefully ignorant of even the most basic of fundamental theories. For God's sake, they don't even know what their own daughter can do. They're quite pathetic, really."

Herrington continued. "Once you get Katie to level fourteen, we should be able to manipulate everything ourselves at that point. Add more stress and she should pop right up to level fifteen. Just like Danny did all those years ago. When we make the switch, she'll be the perfect catalyst until we can get a suitable host."

"How will we make the switch exactly? I'm still not entirely clear on that."

"Once at level fifteen Katie won't even be in this reality any longer. She'll be in a different realm. My theory is her immature mind won't be able to comprehend what's happening to her, and she'll go into shock and simply disappear into the back of her subconscious, the way a child hides behind her mother's skirts when she's scared. She'll still be there, but Marta will be there, too, and should be able to make the jump."

"And Marta will be able to possess her."

"No, not possess. I've told you this already. It will be more like a symbiotic relationship, but one that doesn't benefit the little girl at all. Marta will ride the edge of Katie's consciousness, on the outskirts of her soul, until she can make the switch to a more suitable host. That's where you'll come in. You'll have to arrange to have an empty host waiting for Marta to help her with the jump."

"So, to be clear, the plan still is to kill someone and when their soul leaves, Marta can take over the body?"

Herrington paused. "Perhaps. That's one way. Or, just like when Danny took his parents' and Michael's souls up to his level fifteen he took them from their bodies—someone else with the knowledge could have jumped into them at any time. They were essentially soulless. We could try to replicate that with Marta. This way the host body isn't damaged. I would much prefer it that way."

"Katie won't be soulless? We could simply use her."

"No, the child is powerful. I believe there are some people that can retain their soul regardless if they move up or down. Katie, and Danny, for that matter, can see the other realms while alive, but other people can't. It means they can't be taken over. So Marta will ride along with Katie until we can make the switch."

"And Marta will be prepared?"

"Of course," Herrington said. "I spent hours repeatedly discussing this with her in her final days and now that we know for certain death is not the end point any longer, we can continue in the belief our souls retain an identity. Because of that, it will exist in whatever vessel the soul can reside. Katie will just be the catalyst, and you'll help it all along if you can just get the girl ready. We have already discussed this. You know how much I despise repeating myself."

"I just wanted to be sure. Katie will be ready." There was a pause. "You believe Marta is truly there, down below, waiting for us to get her?"

"I do. She'll understand completely, no matter what type of situation she exists in. She'll know what to do and I'll finally have her back. Now do what you have to do."

If they could pull this off, it would change the world. The fact was they had already discovered the most coveted thing on the planet. The knowledge that the afterlife truly did exist, based on science, not religious, fanatical beliefs. The soul did continue on and did travel with you, but to where and what was the ultimate end question. Soon Marta would be able to tell them intricate details about the other place. Herrington's assistant had no illusions as to which realm Marta went after she died, but it didn't matter. Once she was back, they would use this knowledge, create other machines, and technically be able to live on the human plane for eternity by jumping in and out of bodies whenever they found a vessel to fit their needs. If they could all harness the power Katie had and find some way to give themselves the same gifts, they could find themselves soul-jumping at the very end of every life they led, giving their soul immortality. The possibilities would be limitless for all of them.

It was amazing how much had already been accomplished. Discovering the little girl's abilities, then being able to manipulate the energies while the children were dreaming, and then being able to control the birds in the dreams. It was all about changing the frequencies, linking them to sound and magnetic waves and then utilizing the mind waves of the children to then redirect the birds to do whatever was required. The dark energy field, the black mass, was the coup de grace. The power of all the forces created by using the negative energies of the insects. When connected to that frequency, it created a massive funnel of power and could be manipulated to do whatever bidding was desired. This super energy was being used against the children and the beauty of it was when Danny's birds attacked it, they were killed. And not just killed, but annihilated. When the mass killed a bird outright, the souls inside were unable to do anything. They didn't move on to any light and were unable to go anywhere. They'd just sit there, with no ability to help the Andersons, simply existing in some purgatory world until finally the light would call them again or they started their life over in some other unknown capacity.

And now the children's dreams were no longer safe because the energy could be manipulated into them. Another brilliant concept brought to fruition while Herrington was stuck in a prison cell.

At first, the assistant had been confused at Herrington's wish for Marta to jump into the body of a seven-year-old.

"Why now when Katie is just a child? Why not wait until she's older and her body is more mature? Marta could then just stay in that body."

Herrington had been adamant. "If we wait until Katie's older, she may come into her powers on her own and we won't be able to manipulate them or her. It will be much harder, and with me in jail, I don't have the luxury of a lab to work in. It must be done now while she's young and still naïve to her abilities. At the very worst, Marta will simply have to ride on the edge her consciousness until we find a body for her."

"Will she be able to control Katie?"

"No," Herrington said. "Katie already has a soul and no two bodies can occupy the same soul at one time. Marta will just be sitting on the fringe, waiting. Once she's returned to me, glory awaits us. And don't forget, you're a part of that equation, too."

"Thank you. I appreciate it." The assistant paused. "How are you so certain Marta is down below?"

Herrington had been silent for a long time and the assistant thought he wasn't going to answer. Finally he did. "I never told you this, but only days before the FBI took me away, Marta took a turn for the worse and became delusional. The nurses thought it was the fever speaking because she was rambling, but I knew better. I could tell she was trying to communicate with me and it wasn't just the fever filled dreams talking. When people die, or are about to pass on, many talk about a calmness that comes to their very being. They speak about peace and a bright light and a wondrous feeling of final acceptance.

"Marta did speak about seeing a light, but she was clearly not at peace. She was agitated and kept repeating over and over about seeing a man named Abaddon," Herrington said.

"Abaddon? That's the Hebrew name of Satan, isn't it?"

"Yes, it is," Herrington said.

"And Marta said she saw him?"

"Yes, she told me repeatedly she could see him and he was near her. She claimed he was coming to her room, into her dreams and then she'd ramble on incessantly, referencing the rings of hell. Her descriptions reminded me of Dante's poem."

"Dante's poem? You're talking about the Italian poet, right?"

"One and the same. He wrote a monumental epic poem called The Divine Comedy in the early 1300s, which references the nine circles of Hell. I want you to read up about it when we're done speaking."

The assistant sucked in their breath. "I already know the poem. It supposedly describes Dante as he traveled through Hell, Purgatory, and then ultimately, to Heaven."

Herrington's voice was hushed. "Good, so you do know, but it means much more than that. If you interpret the poem piece by piece it also represents allegorically the soul's journey towards reaching God."

"Wait a second. Are you implying you believe Dante was actually writing about a real place and his travels there and it wasn't just imaginary? How is that possible?"

"It's possible, because I believe he really did take that journey through the nine circles and he was able to fictionalize it as a poem to the world. He was able to describe them to Marta. Perhaps he had the same powers Katie and Danny have when he was alive and traveled there. Perhaps

when he was exiled from Florence he took ill and was close to death to experience this. We have so little historical documentation about him, so we may never know for sure if he committed evil in his life, but I believe he did see this world and it is now where he resides. As to how he did this? It would be anathema of us to think only a little girl can see down below, or only Danny can see up. We must open our minds to the possibilities anyone can learn to travel the realms, as you yourself know. If we tap into these skills, and create machines to heighten awareness, there is no limit to what we can achieve."

"So what happened after Marta told you this?"

"At first I attempted to tell her not to worry, that Abaddon was not real and the circles of Hell were simply literary fiction. But apparently she knew otherwise and she convinced me. She told me Abaddon was coming for her and when she said this to me her eyes were clear. I knew it was not the ramblings of the fever talking. She knew what was going to happen to her and where she was going. She stared me right in the eye and gripped my arm so hard she bruised me and assured me there, indeed, was a hell and she knew she was going there and it was everything everyone thought it was. That she was not destined to go up. She said one final thing to me before she became unresponsive again. She said, "Find me, Samuel. I'll be in the circles waiting for you."

"Those circles can only be in one place—in Dante's version of the underworld. And when we find her, we'll take her from there, right from under Abaddon's nose."

The assistant had been quiet, thinking. "In this place Marta will make the jump. Is it Hell or level fifteen or someplace on the dials in a completely different area?"

Herrington was silent for a moment. "I believe it is the level fifteen in Hell's version of the underworld. The same as Danny's level fifteen for souls before they move on to heaven.

I believe there is the same parallel universe down below. Life is about balance and equality. In Chinese philosophy their notion of the entire universe is based on Yin-Yang."

"Oh, yes. Those black and white circles that meet in the middle. Tell me more."

"The black and white circles represent all actions that occur in the world," Herrington explained. "The yin is dark and passive. The yang is light and active. The middle is where they meet and where everything interacts. I believe this is where our souls can work together with yin-yang and co-exist.

"So—," the stranger said, "—the outer circles represent everything in existence while the two inner connecting circles, the black and the white, represent the interaction of the two energies?"

"Yes, exactly," Herrington said. "This interaction is what causes everything to actually happen. They are intertwined and one cannot exist without the other. I believe it is the same with Danny and Katie. Their powers are the yin-yang of each other. One up, one down. One light, one dark. They are like concentric circles as well and together they can co-exist and reach each other. I believe when you work on them in their dreams, it is yin-yang at its finest. A continual movement of energies."

"Which is why when the mass comes to Katie, the temperature drops," the stranger said.

"Yes, yin-yang. Things can expand and contract, like your breath, in and out, and like temperature, one drops, the other rises. Birds and insects, light and darkness, a young girl and a young boy—these children are the very yin-yang that will bring Marta back. It all flows in a pattern that can be mathematically proven and justified. If we look to yin-yang, Marta may exist in the outer yin circle, but when we get down there and she senses us, she should be able to move to where the two co-exist. I believe that can happen as all energies meet

in the middle. Based on these existing theoretical principles, she should be able to make the jump."

It was only a matter of time before the real show would begin. Once this experiment worked, people could be brought back to life. There would exist the ability to find their souls no matter which plane of existence they resided and simply bring them back up—or down. Chills ran up the assistant's arms at the implication. Herrington had said they'd be an unstoppable team.

The worker glanced up at the sky. It was starting to snow. The news had predicted a sudden, early nor'easter coming to this part of upstate New York.

Excellent. All the pieces were coming together perfectly.

Chapter Eleven

The next morning during breakfast everyone was quiet and solemn. Even Katie, usually so talkative, just ate her cereal with her face close to her bowl. Danny tried to pretend things were normal, but seeing his sister's hands and arms covered in bandages made him lose his appetite. His cornflakes tasted like cardboard. He couldn't imagine his birds would ever do something like this to her. It didn't make any sense. They were good people, even if they were part of a dream. Something had caused them to do what they did and attack her. Something bad. It had to be the mass or some other energy making them react that way. But it was just a dream. How could that even be possible?

After everyone had gone back to sleep the night before, Danny had taken himself straight to level fifteen, speaking to anyone he could, but all he learned was there had been some sort of disturbance of energy that was felt across every level. The beings at level fifteen had distinctly sensed something hostile pulling at them, calling them from far away, but when they realized it was a malevolent pull, they didn't answer. Unfortunately, the ones who most recently passed on, or who were at the very lowest levels of the spectrum, couldn't resist the pull. The birds at level fifteen told him eventually the charge disappeared as if a switch had been turned off and the pull was gone.

"This pull, where was it coming from and what was it exactly?" he had asked.

The birds didn't know where it came from, but this unique energy signature, this hostile wave, was felt not just on level fifteen, but across every level. The enormity and breadth of capacity of its reach concerned them. It wasn't a normal course of events and it was coming from the human realm where he existed. The only other time they had ever experienced that kind of strength was when Maddy would work with Danny on the machine. Or, when Danny called to them as well. But Danny's pull was entirely different. It felt natural, moral and they could ascertain he was using his own electromagnetic abilities, versus something man-made.

Man-made. That made sense, but only to a point. Danny's mother hadn't used the machine the night before and it was locked up tight in the basement. He'd seen her do it himself. No, something else was working on them, making them do things they never would. Danny took a spoonful of cereal and chewed, not even tasting the food. He had to figure this out.

Charity stared at the family and then at Katie's and Danny's arms, her eyebrows raised in confusion. "Um, are you guys okay? I hope I'm not being too forward, but what exactly happened last night?"

Unspoken words flew around the table. Charity wasn't family. How much did they say?

Michael answered her. "Katie had a nightmare last night. She sleepwalked into the bathroom and broke a glass and got cut up pretty badly. Danny tried to help her and got hurt as well." His gaze darted and his face reddened as he said this. Man, his brother was the worst liar on the planet, but at least Charity bought it. "At least you're looking better, Charity."

Danny watched his brother stare at his girlfriend's face. The welts on them had finally receded. A look of relief was stamped on Michael's features.

Michael stared at his own hands, covered with the remnants of bee stings. He cocked his head and grinned. Danny knew the look. His brother was getting ready to make a joke.

"You know, Charity, it's pretty dangerous hanging out with me and my family. Accidents and crazy things seem to follow the Andersons. Like we're magnets for poltergeists or demons or something. Seriously, if we keep dating, you're taking your life into your own hands, and I won't be held responsible if something happens to you."

Chastity stared at Michael and smiled slyly. "Are you trying to scare me off, Michael Anderson? A few bee stings and strange welts on your brother and sister isn't enough to frighten me away. And you should know, I took one full year of Kenpo Karate during high school. I'm a totally super tough chick." Smugly, she took a sip of milk and then started laughing and within seconds she was coughing, choking and milk spewed from her nose.

Michael handed her a napkin, shaking his head and grinning like an idiot as Charity doubled over and coughed violently into the napkin. He patted her back until she got under control, but couldn't stop laughing. "Yeah, you're one tough chick, all right. You better be careful, they say milk is really dangerous, too. You don't have a lactose intolerance or something I don't know about, do you?"

Danny stared at Michael's face and realized something. This wasn't just some girlfriend his brother had brought home. This was serious and different than anything he'd seen in him before. Michael treated Charity as if she were the greatest thing on the planet, and he realized his brother, even after only dating this girl for a few months, was in love. He closed his eyes as his brother leaned in and gave Charity, who could finally breathe again, a quick kiss, to the grinning expressions from his parents and to Katie's squeals of disgust. Danny slurped the milk from his bowl, resigned to having to deal with this while he was eating his breakfast.

Michael glanced out the window. At least a foot of snow already lay on the ground. "I can't imagine the trains are running today. I guess someone might have to stay another night. That's so unfortunate, isn't it?"

"Oh, if I have to, I have to. I'll just have to suffer through it," Charity said, grabbing his hand.

Great. Danny realized Charity wasn't going anywhere. Again, he wouldn't be able to talk to his brother.

Girls.

It continued to snow the entire afternoon and all of them had to remain inside. Maddy had checked everyone's radiation levels and they were in the normal range, which surprised her so much she spent most of the afternoon in her office in the basement recalibrating the device and the machine to make sure there weren't any anomalies. Gary spent the afternoon opening up the floor vent in the basement to run tubing and a snake through it to see if there were any traces of the apparition Danny and Katie had told him about. His face was grim as he brought up bucket loads of dead bugs, worms, and mucky leaves. The smell was vile. Gary spent the next few hours running tests on the material to see if they were anything other than what they appeared to be.

Katie took Danny aside that night before they went to bed. "I'm scared to go to sleep. Bad things happen to me when I'm sleeping."

He nodded, knowing what she meant. "Mom and Dad will be right next to you. You'll be safe and they'll help you if something happens."

She crinkled her nose. "Yeah, like last night? They can't help me when I'm dreaming."

No, they couldn't. Maybe he could. "Look, if we're both dreaming the same things, I've heard about something called shared dreaming or how people can control their dreams. I think it's called lucid dreaming. I don't know enough about it yet, but what I do know is there are ways for us to control our dreams and if we both learn how to do it, maybe we can fight against the mass when it comes into our nightmares. Maybe we can recognize it and tell each other we're dreaming and we can wake ourselves up."

She seemed unconvinced. Danny brought her to their parents' room, pausing before the new camera clicking in the corner.

He tucked her into the bed. "If we stick together, we should be okay." He stayed with her a few more minutes until she started to drift off and then went back into Michael's room.

No matter that they talked, and no matter that there were videos to watch and record everything, that night Danny's nightmare was the worst it had ever been.

He was back in Magnolia Fields and Katie was again at his side. He and Katie strolled through the field, his footsteps soft on the soggy ground as if it had just rained, but the sun was bright. Too bright, and it made little flashes of light as it glinted off his pendant. Katie stooped to pick up little fragrant wildflowers and raised one to her nose and sniffed. An eight-inch blue butterfly swooped down to her and she put out her hand. It alighted on her fingertips, opening and closing its wings. With a sudden shudder, it took to the sky. Katie stared after it, her brow furrowed. "It's scared."

"Scared of what?" Danny signed.

Katie turned and glanced towards the woods. "Of me going in there. He knows I'm going to have to go into the trees."

Danny shook his head. "I don't want you going in there. It's dangerous in the woods, Katie. The tornado is in there."

"The tornado is everywhere, Danny. We can't hide from it." She suddenly grimaced and put her hand to her head.

"What's the matter? Are you okay? Are you having another headache?" He grabbed her arm.

She pushed him away and took two hesitant steps towards the forest. Her eyes widened. "My headache is going away a little." She took two more steps.

"Katie, stop. I'm telling you that you can't go in there. Please, I know what's happening. We're dreaming again." When he uttered the words, it felt right. They were dreaming and they were together, but they could feel. He pinched his arm. Yes, he could feel pain. Katie could have her headaches. Somehow this dream world was real. "Wake yourself up, Katie. Right now, try to wake yourself up." He grabbed his sister's arm again and this time shook her.

She whimpered a little and her legs faltered. "I can't. My head is starting to hurt bad again." She brushed off his grip and took another step towards the forest. "Whenever I walk towards the trees, my headache leaves a little." She paused for a second more and her eyes widened as a rush of static, like a mini electric charge, brushed by him. His sister smiled widely, relief stamped on her face. "Oh, yeah. That works, too. That feels even better."

More charges in the air brushed by him. One, two, three—whisking past him whippet fast and the hair on his arms stood up. He knew this feeling. It was the same feeling he had when he turned on the lights using the machine or took himself to level fifteen. She was pushing?

"Are you pushing right now? Are you making rustles with your mind? You have to stop."

"I'm just getting rid of my headache. When I make the little rustles, it makes them better. I didn't know I could do that."

It was as if she were moving up the levels on the machine all by herself. He had to stop her. If she were moving up the dials, she was also going to bring bad things and that meant they would come in the dream and possibly at home, too, while they were sleeping. What number was she even on now?

"How many rustles did you make, Katie?" Another charge whisked by him. He grabbed his sister's arms again and squeezed a little. "Katie, stop it. You have to wake yourself up. Don't make the rustles anymore or we're going to get hurt. I don't care if you have a headache, you have to stop." He looked around, frantically. "I'll try to help us wake up." He craned his head to the sky and called for his birds. He closed his mind to focus on the part that reached for them and he pushed, but when he did, nothing happened. Calling his birds over the years had become as easy as breathing, but now, like the other night in his bedroom when the mass had attacked him and his sister, nothing happened. He tried again, but couldn't make even the smallest rustle. He felt like a magician who had lost his wand. Of course, this was just a dream, so why would they come, right? Frustrated, he turned back to his sister, who had moved closer to the forest, step by step, until all that separated her from the woods was a patch of grass.

She turned to him, her face pained. "I have to go in there, Danny. Something's calling me." She suddenly bolted forwards and disappeared into the woods.

Startled, Danny raced after her, but it was dark within the trees. The branches loomed overhead, the canopy stretching and blocking out any sunlight as if he were deep in the Amazon rainforest. His feet tread over dead leaves and soggy mush. The ground smelled of rot and mold. He stopped running and turned his body in circles, desperately searching for his sister. He couldn't see her anywhere. The hair on his arms stood up and he felt the energy whisk by him, this time stronger than before and he turned towards it. Her powers were growing. He tried to follow the trail, but got distracted. Shadows darted past him and he felt something hard thump against his leg, as if Michael had kicked him underneath the kitchen table. Danny glanced down to his calf, but nothing was there. Pain shook him when something else punched him in his arm and then again in his jaw and he cried out and dropped to his knees. Another charge whisked by him and something sharp and prickly scraped across his cheek. Danny flailed at the air and tried to hit whatever was attacking him. Black wisps resembling sheer black handkerchiefs flew around him in a circle and his skin seemed to freeze as each one brushed against him as if they were made of ice.

"Kateee, fight it," he called out desperately as best he could. "Stop making rustles." He didn't even know if she could hear him or understand him. What level was she on now anyway?

A bright, pulsing red light, the color of blood, flickered in the forest ahead. It was distant, but he saw it through the apparitions flying in circles around him. He stood and tried to push himself through them, but they condensed together in a frigid wall, keeping him from the light—trying to stop him from finding his sister. Danny pressed forward, into them, as if moving through sludge and their icy coldness enveloped his body and momentarily stunned him. With sheer will he struggled through, his breath being taken away, but he felt them weaken, and blessed warm air rushed into him as he tore past and through the forest towards the red light.

The woods thinned and opened out into a small clearing and that's where he found his sister, kneeling on the ground and clutching her head. He ran to her and pulled her into his arms, wrapping his arms around her protectively. Smoke demons whisked by them and flew around them. The air became colder and colder until they could see their breath steaming in the air.

"I tried to stop the rustles, but then my head started hurting. Please make them go away." She moaned and buried her head in his chest.

He covered his sister with his body as more of the beings hit him and he shook as an electric charge pulsed through him. He glanced at Katie, her eyes clear and knew her headache had lessened. She had made the rustle and gone up another level. He was terrified of what was going to happen next, because there was absolutely nothing he could do to fight what might come.

Katie started hyperventilating and her eyes widened in understanding. "It's me. I know what I'm doing. I just wanted to stop my headache, but it's coming now." Her eyes were wide with panic.

"What's coming?" She didn't have to answer as the black mass floated into the clearing. It resembled a dark, malignant cloud. The smell was overwhelming and, in the depths of the rotating mass, he could see pieces of dead things coagulating and turning inside. It was like looking at the guts of a person.

He signed to his sister. "Can you send it away? Can you turn off the rustles, one by one and make it disappear?"

"I don't know how." She clutched at him, unable to answer and buried her face back against his chest. Maybe if they were home, maybe if they were not in this situation, he could teach her, but here there was nothing he could do.

"Wake up. Wake up. Wake up," he willed himself, but nothing happened. He sat helpless as the mass advanced until it was only a few feet from them and he felt himself go numb. His sister shivered violently in his arms. Standing up, his teeth chattering, he pushed Katie protectively behind him. 'You can't have her," he thought out to the mass. He tried to feel it. Tried to reach it, and for the first time felt something emanate from it and heard it in his head clear as day. They had finally linked together.

It was sending dark, evil thoughts. Thoughts of pain and of suffering. His mind reeled from the horrific images it sent into him and his knees nearly buckled.

Katie must have felt it, too. She clenched him tighter.

He saw darkness and horror. Deformed and wretched souls. People imbedded in ice, people burning, rivers of boiling blood and fire, and violent sandstorms. Image after horrible image was shown upon him like movie clips sped up on a reel.

He was certain this thing was not from above, not from the world of oneness where the souls came together. Not from a land of beautiful fields and love and peace. This was from below. From a land where every being suffered in their own miserable, singular existence.

It spoke to him. "She's ours." The mass pounded its message in his head and he realized like when he was at level fifteen and could hear the birds, he could hear this being, too. He shot a message back to it.

"You can't have her."

His mind filled with maniacal laughter that shook him to his very core. He tried to call to his birds, but he couldn't feel them. He tried to wake himself up, to hit himself, but it was as if he were chained or drugged, stuck in a cell with no escape.

The mass rippled, as if mocking him and then it spoke to him, his entire mind filled with one thought.

"You can't do anything, Danny. You will lose."

It knew his name. He squeezed his sister harder.

Then the mass attacked, covering them both.

They were falling fast down a dark, dank shaft, twisting and turning violently, like Alice in Wonderland as she fell through the rabbit hole. Danny clutched his sister in his arms, hugging her so fiercely he thought he might crush her, but there was no way he was letting go. Their bodies banged and flailed into the sides. Jagged rocks ripped into their skin and they plunged down into an endlessly deep pit. From below he could see sparks of reds and yellows, and he smelled smoke, sulfur, and ash. He could hear and heard his sister screaming.

They hit an outcropping of rock jutting from the wall and with a thud, they landed on it hard. His breath was knocked out of him. Katie lay on top of him, shaking uncontrollably. The ledge was small and their bodies were balanced precariously on it. One false move and they would fall. With one hand, he desperately clutched at the rock behind him while holding onto his sister with his other hand. Katie put her hands to her head and he saw her moan. Her headache was back and it was bad.

Her brow crinkled. She glanced up and he felt her body prickle and charge, like a Van De Graf Generator. She sighed in relief as her headache disappeared. He tensed, knowing without a doubt more bad things were coming.

The rock ledge started to break apart and hideously distorted and deformed beings from below shot up from the depths of the inferno and flew in circles, surrounding them.

"I have to wake up. I have to wake up." How many times had he tried? He squeezed his sister to him, willing her to wake up with his mind. "Katie, it's just a dream. Wake up." He tried to link to her mind, but it was like he was hitting a brick wall he couldn't penetrate. He couldn't feel anything from her but her fear.

The rock ledge collapsed and down they plunged. Down and down, falling fast. Below them a black beast appeared and the closer they fell, the larger and more hideous it became. Katie screamed when she saw the beast's wide open mouth. Danny could see the pointed, rotted fangs, the swollen tongue, the yellow eyes as they dropped into its maw and then they went through it and into it, bringing them to a place no longer in the well.

In a moment they entered a world so alien to him, so foreign, he couldn't process it at first. They were in a deep gorge of darkness with dead trees and animal carcasses riddling the blackened floor. People milled about, but they were hunched over. Their knuckles dragged over the dirt, as if they had been carrying heavy loads for centuries and were physically deformed by it. Raging fires exploded around them and he could feel his skin burn from the intense heat. Putrid smelling rivers of sludge appeared and lapped at their feet and burned anything that touched it. Danny grabbed his sister, pulled her away and they ran blindly through a ground made of smoke and ash. Beasts circled around them, mocking, ridiculing, and taunting them as they tried to find their way out.

"Help me." He called out to anyone and anything that would listen.

Then he saw it. A faint white light, a mere dot in the landscape, showed itself in the far reaches of a blood red sky. Danny felt the black presence scream in fury. He didn't know if the white dot was always there or if he just noticed it, but once he saw it, he knew it could save them. He propelled Katie towards it.

Beings grabbed and pulled at them, trying to stop them from going to the light. Katie fell to her knees and Danny scooped her in his arms. The beasts tore at his clothing, scorched his skin, and ripped his shirt and necklace from his body.

Danny appealed to the light and suddenly it brightened so magnificently, it lit the dark land like rays from sunbeams breaking through the clouds. With banshee wails that screeched in his head, the beings fled. Enraged, the black mass raced towards him and tried to block his way.

Little dots shot out of the light and streaked towards him. They were birds, each glowing with the power from above. Danny called to them desperately and they stormed directly into the mass. In a fury the mass expanded, tripled and quadrupled in size. This was its domain. This was where its power was strongest. There was no way they could win and Danny could feel that knowledge in the birds, but it didn't matter. They were there for one thing only. Not to save themselves, but to save him and his sister.

"Run," they ordered.

He ran. With a leap that could only be made in dreams, he took a step and jumped, holding onto his sister desperately as they flew across the plains and soared directly into the bright light.

They were gone.

Danny landed on the floor next to the bed thrashing, the blankets and his sleep clothes in a twisted heap around him. Michael stooped over to help him, but Danny pushed his brother violently aside. He lurched to his feet, raced into his parent's room and turned on the lights.

"Danny, what are you doing? Where are your clothes?" his mother signed, squinting at him.

He had time only to notice he was in his boxers before he blurted out. "Where's Katie?" He ripped the covers off the bed, staring at the empty space between his parents.

His mother sat up, her mouth ajar. "Oh, my God, she's not here." His parents shot out of bed. "What happened? Did you have another dream? Your arms are burned, and your hair is covered with soot."

He saw his reflection in the mirror and reeled back. He didn't look like himself, didn't look rational. It didn't matter. What mattered was finding his sister. "The dreams are real and I know how all these bad things are coming. Katie's doing it."

The family searched the second floor, calling for their daughter and when they didn't find her, they tried downstairs.

Michael searched outside, Maddy to the basement. Gary checked the garage, but Katie was gone.

They met in the kitchen. Maddy's hands were on her cell phone ready to call 911 when Charity came out of the guest room off the kitchen, yawning and rubbing her eyes. "Hey, what's going on?"

"Have you seen Katie?" Michael asked, as his mother started dialing.

Charity nodded. "Yeah, she's sleeping in my room."

Maddy stopped dialing and put the phone back on the counter. "She's in your room?"

Charity nodded. "She said she had a bad dream and came downstairs to get something to drink. I gave her some milk and she was practically falling asleep so I put her in the other bed in the guest room with me. I didn't want to go upstairs and wake you guys. That was okay, right?"

The Andersons converged into the guestroom. Katie was sleeping soundly on the extra bed. Danny moved over to her, his jaw clenched. Katie held her head as if it hurt. She had scratches on her face, a huge bruise on her arm and red burn marks on her bare legs. Her feet were black with soot. He turned to Charity accusingly.

"Didn't you see she was hurt?"

Charity shrugged, confused. "I just thought they were the same injuries from the other day. Did something else happen to her?"

Danny advanced on her, ready to tell her off and Michael grabbed him. "Hey, Danny, lay off her. It's not Charity's fault. She was just trying to help."

"Of course she was," Maddy said soothingly. "No one is saying otherwise. Charity, thank you for taking care of her and helping her get back to sleep. We appreciate it. Gary, let's take Katie and Danny back upstairs and clean them up. I want to watch the videos and see what happened."

Gary bent and took Katie in his arms. She woke up and started crying and yelling about scary people and tornadoes.

Gary patted her head and tried to soothe her as they all moved back upstairs, except for Michael who stayed downstairs with Charity to smooth things over.

As their mother and father treated their burns and cleaned them up, yet again, Danny and Katie told them about the dream.

Maddy took Katie's chin in her hands. "Honey, can you control making those rustles? Can you stop doing them if you have to?"

Katie shook her head, sniffling. Her eyes were bloodshot and her nose was running from crying. "If I stop, my headache starts hurting me again."

Gary leaned in and rubbed at her nose with a tissue. "Maybe we can give her medication to stop the headaches? Possibly a migraine drug?"

Michael walked into the room, shaking his head. "I wouldn't do that. We drug her, and then she'll be nothing but a pawn for whatever is after her. She'll be unconscious and it will attack her in her dream with no recourse. Maybe if she's not drugged she can find some way to control it." He turned to Danny. "It took you someplace this time?"

Danny was still mad at Michael, but had calmed down enough to speak to his brother civilly. "We went into one of the demons and they took us to a dead land."

"It looked like a scary, haunted moon, Mommy," Katie said.

Danny nodded. "Worse than the moon. Filled with millions of gross things and exploding fires and flames."

"And creepy people," Katie chimed in.

Danny nodded. "We were only there for a short time, but it's pretty horrible."

"How did you get out of it?" Maddy asked. "How did you escape?"

"There was this light in the sky," Danny said. "At first it was just a tiny little dot. I don't know if it was always there or just showed up, but it was there and when I called out to it and begged for help, it seemed to hear me. The light got bigger and birds came out and flew into the black mass that was trying to hold us back. Those birds saved us."

"The light was able to show you a way out of there? It was there in that realm?" Maddy glanced at Gary. "So there is a link between the two afterlifes? They must be connected after all."

Michael cocked his head. "Well, some religious history claims the two realms are related. Isn't there an old fable that says they were once run by two brothers? There's always a grain of truth to those old tales."

Gary shook his head. "True, but other stories say the underworld is run by Satan who was one of God's angels and who tricked Adam and Eve."

Maddy nodded. "Whatever the case, I believe our lives don't end just because our human existence does. We now have proof we go someplace. The question is, ultimately, where? So the birds, in your dream, were able to penetrate that land and the light appeared and got you out of there. The light actually sought you out and protected you."

Danny interrupted his mother. "Yes, but, Mom, I was dreaming. It wasn't real."

Gary chimed in. "True, but dreams can feel real and there are tales that they can create physical manifestations, such as the injuries you both have. The question is, why do you think you were finally able to reach your birds, Danny? Why, at that moment, and not any other time when you called for their aid? Through all that is happening to you, you've told me repeatedly your abilities are disappearing at times. Do you know why?"

He shook his head. He didn't know. One moment he couldn't summon any abilities, and the next he could. It made no sense to him.

His mother touched his arm. "If you had to guess, what level is she up to, Danny?"

He swallowed. Based on how far they'd gone and what he'd seen and the beings she'd summoned? "I don't know, Mom, but I'll bet it's close to nine or even ten. Geez, it could be higher. I felt charge after charge and the beings kept getting stronger. Stronger than anything I've seen yet." He stared at his sister, wondering how in the world she had gotten there so fast.

As Danny fell back to sleep that night, he felt they finally knew more than they ever did before, while still knowing absolutely nothing.

Chapter Twelve

The next morning brought clear skies, but frigid air. Reports of iced-over roads and dangerous driving conditions filled the news. Railroads and subways were down and everyone was advised to stay indoors. That was fine with Michael. He and Charity went up to his room and shut the door. Seconds later Danny saw his mother rolling her eyes and telling his father to please ask Michael to turn down his stereo.

His parents had watched the videos and seen Katie tossing and turning while they slept. At one point she woke up, eased out of bed and walked down the stairs. She was holding her head the entire time. What terrified them was her breath steaming in the air, as if it were freezing in the house, which it wasn't. It looked like something cold and dead was following her.

Danny took his sister aside while his parents debated the tapes.

"We need to talk."

She stared up at him. "Mommy is taking me to the lab tomorrow. She wants to do some tests on me. Does she think I'm sick and that's why I have these bad headaches?"

Danny shook his head. "No, she doesn't. I think she's going to do some tests to figure out how you're going up the dials on a machine without even having one in front of you."

She bit her lip. "You know how I talk to my bug friends and it's always happy talk, like I do with Mickey? My insects don't hurt me, but certain bugs do. When they come to me, they hurt my head and unless I do something about it, it hurts more."

"Does it hurt now?"

She shook her head no.

He wondered something. Dreams were one thing, but could she do it at will? "Can you make a rustle with your mind without it hurting first?"

She crinkled her nose. "Aren't you scared of me bringing bad things?"

He cocked his head. "No, we won't go high. We'll just practice. See if you can make a light rustle."

Katie concentrated and pushed a little and Danny felt the charge. Katie's eyes widened. "Oh, I can."

"Do you have a headache?"

She shook her head no.

So when she did it herself, there was no pain. "Try again, Katie."

She squinted her brows in concentration and then another charge came and then a third. The air around them got darker. Something thumped lightly against his leg, but it didn't hurt him. A spider crawled out of the wood and skittered towards them.

"Okay, stop, Katie. Don't go any further," he signed. Now that they were home, and not in the bad place, maybe he could teach her how to control them. He could feel the air still charged around him.

"I want you to try to push all the charges away. Take the rustles back like they're lights on the dial and pretend you're turning them off, one by one." He couldn't even gauge what level she was on. He had felt three charges, but was that really just level three? What if each rustle doubled or tripled the levels with her?

"How do I take them back?" She stooped to catch the spider with her hand and it quickly scooted up and down her arm. Another came out of a crack in the wall and rushed across the floor, its legs moving a mile a minute.

Danny stared at the spiders. “Are they saying anything to you?”

She shook her head. “Nothing bad. They just came because I called them.”

Danny felt something whisk by him again. The air was charging still and more spiders crept out from the wall. “Katie, pretend you’re shutting off a lamp. Think of a light switch in your mind and simply turn it off. Watch me and see if you can feel what I do.” He pushed a little and felt his own powers growing, felt other things flicker in the air and Katie stared at him in awe. Shadows surrounded them, but from both ends of the spectrum. Some dark and some light. The shadows flew into each other, around each other, comingling, as if competing for the space. Good and bad together. “Now, push yours away, like you’re closing off a light switch one by one. Watch me, so you can feel what I’m doing.” He pushed with his mind and his shadows slowly disappeared.

She closed her eyes and concentrated. Danny knew it was working. The light around him slowly brightened and the hair on his arms didn’t tingle as much.

“A little more, Katie. Turn them all off.”

Katie crinkled her brow and finally turned to him, smiling. “I turned them all off.” She put the spider on the floor and he and his partner scurried back behind the wall with the others.

“You did really good.” He was relieved she could do it herself and amazed at the same time. Now, the question was, why couldn’t he help all the time? Why could he only sometimes connect to his powers and other times not? And more importantly, why were her sister’s powers growing so fast and seemingly so strong? It was the one major piece of the puzzle he was missing.

An idea struck him. It was a terrible one, but made such sense, it terrified him to no end. “Katie, I’ll be right back.

Don't do any more rustles. Not even for fun, okay?" He ran upstairs and burst into Michael's room. He and Charity were making out on his bed and he coughed into his hand, embarrassed.

Michael turned to him, annoyed. "Hey, don't you ever knock?"

Danny stared at Charity, who was nuzzling his brother's neck. "Michael, I have to talk to you. Now. In private."

Michael looked exasperated and Charity moved out of his arms. "Right now you need to talk to me? Seriously? Can't this wait?"

"No, it can't."

"What do you want to talk about?" Michael glared at him.

Danny glanced at Charity, stalling.

"I'm not making Charity leave. You're the one who burst in here. Now spill it, Birdman. You want to talk to me, then talk."

Danny scowled. "Fine, I want to talk to you about Samuel Herrington."

Michael squinted. He frowned and sat up. "What about him?"

Charity wrinkled her nose in obvious distaste. "That evil scientist who's in jail? The one who tried to hurt you guys?"

Michael turned to her, surprised. "You know about him? Why didn't you ever tell me?"

Charity rolled her eyes. "Yeah, like I'm going to bring up that horrible man when you're asking me out on a date. And, not to mention you're like this huge b-list celebrity in the lab. Everyone told me who you were the first day I started classes and everything else that happened to you guys. I didn't say anything because I didn't want you to think I was only dating you because you're quasi-famous." She turned to Danny. "You know, you're both really lucky you got away from that man. He's seriously dangerous. I don't care what the news reports. I really think Herrington was the one who poisoned the coral reef and gave all those people in Africa cholera. They're even saying he's responsible for the rise of polio and all these other diseases that have basically been gone from American culture for years, but have made a comeback. I'll bet he's also responsible somehow for all these new cases of autism. I think he's finding a way to get people sick on a whole host of levels."

Michael raised his eyebrows. "I didn't know you thought about this so much. Or even knew so much about him."

She stared at him, exasperated. "We're scientists, Michael. That's what we do. We learn, we study, and we think." She pointed at her head with her finger, pressing it against her temple for emphasis. "I do read the news, you know."

Danny exhaled. It wasn't like Charity was telling him anything he didn't already know. "Michael, is Herrington still in that maximum security prison in Sing Sing?"

Michael nodded. "Of course, he is. The guy's got so many life sentences, we'll be in the next millennia before his turn comes up for parole. Actually, I don't even think he's eligible. Why are you asking me this?"

"Can I please talk to you in private?" he begged.

"I can leave," Charity said, sliding off the bed, but Michael grabbed her arm, staying her.

"No, don't go anywhere. What Danny has to say he can say to both of us." Michael stared at his brother defiantly.

Danny was angry. This was an entirely new angle to their relationship.

"Spill it, Danny."

What else could he do? He had to tell someone what he thought.

"Fine. I think Herrington might be behind what's happening to us."

Michael laughed at him and Danny felt sick to his stomach. "Come on. The guy is hundreds of miles away and locked up with nothing in his cell but a toilet. What can he possibly do to us?"

Deflated, Danny sat on the edge of the bed and put his head in his hands. It was true. Just what could Herrington do to them when he was imprisoned twenty-four hours a day? Absolutely nothing. He didn't know why he brought it up and now his brother thought he was being stupid and a big baby about nothing.

Unless…

He looked up, signing. "But, what if he's somehow able to get information to the outside? I mean, the guy is one of the richest men in the world, so I'm sure he's capable of bribing someone on the inside. He must have connections whether he's in prison or not. You know, he was making a machine, back when he…" He stopped signing and stared at Charity, not sure how much more he should say.

Michael shook his head and leaned towards his brother. "Danny, listen to me carefully. There's no possible way this guy can have anything to do with what's happening with you and Katie. Seriously, you think too much. What do you think he's doing sitting in his small prison cell? You think he has the ability to do work on any experiments or have huge conversations with people about destroying the world? You think he's spending his free time just thinking up ways to get back at you? Trust me, he isn't. Everything he's ever loved has been stripped from him.

"His money is all gone, his wife is dead and he's out of the picture. He's a terrorist in the worst sense of the word and he can't hurt anyone ever again, so please stop worrying. He's not a magician and he isn't God. And the only people he sees are his lawyers who come and go. I don't think they even like the guy. Now go on and get out of here and give Charity and me some privacy. And be cool and fix the gift she gave you. I've never met someone who busted up a stinking necklace so much. You're worse than a girl."

Charity snorted and smacked Michael on the arm. "Thanks a lot, Michael Anderson." She turned to Danny. "It's okay if you don't like it, Danny. I don't mind, really. I can return it. I still have the receipt."

He shook his head, frowning. Like he had time to worry about how his brother's girlfriend would feel if he didn't wear her gift? Geez. "I like it just fine, it just has a way of getting ripped off my body when bad things are happening. Don't worry, I'll tape it back together, again."

"Okay, that's good." Charity giggled as Michael turned back to her.

Danny left the room, glowering and feeling stupid. Well, that had been absolutely no help. He shut the door and headed down the steps.

Gary met him at the bottom rung, his hands filled with videotapes and notebooks. "Dad, Samuel Herrington is still in jail, right?"

His father paused. "Of course, why do you ask?"

Why? Because he thought he had something to do with Katie's powers? Because he thought maybe he built some sort of machine on his own and was somehow, from his prison cell, using it on his sister? It was ridiculous and he was sure his father's response would be just like Michael's.

"Never mind. I was just thinking."

Gary smiled kindly and put his books and tapes down on the first step. He tousled Danny's hair. "I want you to stop worrying about this, okay? It definitely has nothing to do with Herrington. In fact, your mom and I have a theory that wraps everything up perfectly."

Danny groaned. Oh, no. His parents and their endless theories.

Gary went on, oblivious to how his son felt. "We believe all of this has to do with electromagnetic waves and there's some sort of disturbance going on in the atmosphere that is ultimately affecting your sister. She obviously has powers and sensitivities we didn't know about, and now something is either magnifying them or causing a disturbance in the waves that she can feel and it's affecting her."

Danny put up his hand. "Dad, please just make sure you explain this in English, ok?"

Gary raised his eyebrows. "Don't I always? As I was saying, we believe everything that's being triggered is occurring from natural events. In fact, I'm on a conference call in an hour with a group of our cosmologists who are covering a geomagnetic storm presently building in space. It's a biggie and my gut says it's interacting with earth's magnetic field and increasing the amount of energy into the magnetosphere. Of course, we'll have to check the sunspot cycle to see if it's coinciding with that as well, but if it is, we could simply equip Katie with a dampening shield to help her get through it until the worst of it is over. That could be what's messing with your abilities, too, by the way."

Danny sighed. He was always glad his father didn't speak to him like a child like so many of his friends' parents did, but still, there were limits to how much he understood. "Dad, electromagnetism in the atmosphere? What does that even mean?"

Gary exhaled and then thought for a moment. "Okay, think of a big wind of energy getting pushed towards earth. It's just like a wave racing to the shoreline, but this one is a wave rippling from space right down through the air and straight to your sister. If that's the case, it could be interacting with Katie's abilities and causing all sorts of problems with her insect friends. And, your birds would be affected as well as they could also feel this big wind of energy. It would mess up the electromagnetic waves for all of them."

That made sense. Unfortunately, his father had more to say on the topic. "The question to ask is if Katie is causing the mass and other things to happen because of the interaction or is the interaction causing these things to happen? It's the circular cause and consequence theory at its finest."

Danny groaned and his dad laughed. "Sorry. I should have just said it's the chicken or the egg scenario. We just don't know which scenario is first or second." He touched his son's arm and squeezed him affectionately.

Danny crinkled his brows worriedly. "So you don't think Katie is bringing us to the underworld any longer?"

Gary shook his head. "No, I really don't think so. I think you're both having nightmares and creating this place with some sort of linked mind wave. I could be wrong, and scientists should always keep an open mind, but let's see if this idea pans out and if it does, we can adjust things and maybe the nightmares will simply go away. Try not to worry. We're on top of it."

Danny couldn't just ignore what he was thinking. He had to make his father understand what he believed. "Dad, I'm sorry, but I don't think it's just sunspot activity. I really do believe there are other places besides my level fifteen and I think Katie is physically causing these things to happen. It's like she's working on a machine all by herself and moving up the dials super-fast."

Gary's eyes widened in bewilderment. "It's not possible, Danny. Your mother locked up the machine. There's just no way for Katie to become so strong and work on her abilities by herself. She's too young, and she hasn't even been trained in what to look for. There's no way on her own she could achieve the magnitude of what's been happening. You guys were just dreaming, and lucid dreaming to boot, but that's all it was. Once we know what's happening to her, we'll begin in earnest to control it. I'm sure we'll be able to settle everything soon."

Danny bit his lip, biting off a sarcastic retort. Yeah, that's what all this was. Just sunspot activity. That's why they were getting bloodied and bruised in the middle of the night and his room got destroyed by a malevolent beast. He stared at his father, wondering if he should even ask. Oh, why not? He'd already been embarrassed by Michael. "So you don't think Herrington is involved?" he signed.

Gary's jaw dropped. "How could he possibly be involved in what's happening?"

"Well, wasn't he making his own machine once?"

Gary nodded, measuring his words. "Yes…he was, but the FBI found that machine when we captured him and confiscated it. In fact, your mother and I examined it and it was useless. All it did was work with sound waves, which have nothing to do with anything substantial in the electromagnetic spectrum. Maybe we could link it somehow with frequencies only insects can sense, but that's really the only unique feature about it. He was completely off base with what he thought we were doing. Now that he's in jail and his wife is dead, he has no one else to work with him."

"You don't think he could bribe someone to help him? Get someone else to make another machine?

Gary shook his head. "Even if they could, why would they? And how could they? Herrington has no access to anyone. Danny—son—please know he can't hurt you or any of us anymore. He's monitored twenty-four hours a day and he's had no visitors except for his lawyers on and off for the past seven years. While there's always corruption in places, this one isn't it. The FBI is personally invested in this man and constantly checks in, with the entire goal to keep us safe.

Herrington just doesn't have any power over us anymore. I don't even think about him, so please don't worry."

"Okay, Dad." Trying not to worry would be easier said than done. Basically his father had just confirmed to him something strange was going on, but he was still not entirely convinced a solar magnetowhateverthingie was causing it. He still thought it was something much worse, but apparently no one else did.

He sighed and went to find his sister.

Chapter Thirteen

At four o'clock, they had a blackout.

Danny was in the family room watching television with Katie when the screen and the lights flickered and then shut off. His mom walked into the room, her hands on her hips.

"Well, it was only a matter of time before that happened," Maddy said. "I felt like we were living on borrowed time with what the news has been reporting. We certainly can't stay here tonight, that's for sure. The heat is off, it's thirty degrees outside and unless we find the candles and flashlights we won't be able to even talk to Danny after the next thirty minutes. So, let's get packed before it gets too dark and head over to the lab. We'll grab one of the visitor bungalows. It'll be tight, but they have a generator back-up system and we'll be warm for the evening."

Michael and Charity ambled into the room as she was talking. She nodded to Michael. "Go grab some extra blankets, and Danny, please get together a change of clothes for you and Katie. Oh, and don't forget your toothbrushes." She glanced at Charity. "I guess you finally get to go home, dear. There's just no room for you at the lab. It's been absolutely lovely having you, although I'm sorry about quite a few things. We'll have to make it up to you the next time you visit."

Charity smiled. "It's okay, Mrs. Anderson. It's definitely been interesting, I'll say that for sure. Michael can just drop me off at the train station, since they're running. I'm pretty sure it comes every hour so there won't be any problems. I have the schedule in here somewhere." She started rummaging in one of her bag's many pockets to find the timetable. Tissues and old receipts spilled onto the floor.

The family separated to go do their separate chores and pack up for the night to go to the lab. Bundled up in hats, gloves, scarves and the like, Maddy put Katie in her booster seat as Gary got the heat going. Danny hopped into the backseat of Michael's car, moving aside the fast food wrappers and textbooks covering it.

Michael turned around to face him, his hands about to put the key into the ignition. He didn't seem pleased to see him. "Danny, can't you drive with mom and dad? I'll be along right after I drop Charity off."

Charity was next to Michael in the front seat and hid her smile behind her gloved hands.

Danny scowled. He knew Michael wanted to be alone with his girlfriend, but this way after he dropped Charity off, he'd finally get the chance to talk to him. "I'll just sit here and be quiet and won't even look at the two of you. You can make all the stupid gooey talk you like. It's not like I'll hear you anyway."

Michael made a face at him in the mirror, and then with a teasing grin, leaned over and gave Charity a very big kiss. Disgusted, Danny sat back and endured the ride to the train station.

Michael waited with Charity in the depot until the train came, while Danny jumped into the front seat and tried to ignore their goodbyes. As the train pulled away Michael climbed into the car and started the trip to their parent's lab, thirty minutes away. It was housed on the grounds of a now defunct university, which had shut its doors during the First World War. The company that had purchased it, Hi Core Industries, had massively increased the size of the complex, moving deeper and deeper into the woods as they expanded the facility. Frowning, Michael glanced at Danny as they rode.

"Okay, so are you going to tell me what your problem is? Why don't you like Charity? What did she ever do to you?"

Danny fingered the necklace around his neck as he lip-read. "I like her just fine," he signed.

Michael raised his eyebrows. "Oh, really? Well, you don't act like it. All she's ever done is be nice to you. You've been a real jerk around her."

Danny glared at him. "Well, maybe that's because you get all weird when she's around and I needed to talk to you. I mean, crazy stuff is happening and it's like you don't even care."

Michael raised his brows. "Don't care? That's completely unfair. My girlfriend sees a crazy poltergeist come to the house, your floor gets covered by dead birds, she gets viciously attacked by an infestation of bees, we have this freak snowstorm so she can't even get home and you're upset I'm giving her some attention? Are you serious? Come on, Danny. You're being ridiculous. Not everything is always about you, you know." He signed one-handed and spoke to him, clearly upset.

Danny looked at him, chagrined and stared at his hands.

Michael softened and patted his brother's head through the snow hat and then tugged on his chin, so he'd look up at him. "Look, I know things have been hard, and I'm sorry I wasn't here for most of it. But, I'm here now. Charity's on her way back to New York City and I'm around for another few days. I'm sure we'll figure out what's going on. Dad thinks it simply has to do with some solar conditions, and if we can calibrate the waves to match what's happening with Katie and do an adjustment on her, maybe whatever she's channeling will just go away and everything will go back to normal. The two of you are just wired differently from other people, and if we can figure out what's making her tick, just like Mom and Dad learned with you, we'll get it all under control."

"And the fact that we're dreaming the same thing?" Danny asked. "And that we're getting hurt in our dreams?"

"Same concept. They'll do an adjustment on you, too. Maybe this shift in space is also what's been giving you these nightmares. Something in the atmosphere causing you guys to react to what's in your dreams."

"Wait, so you think we're personally hurting ourselves, because we're reacting to something?"

Michael shrugged. "It's possible. You thrash around and dig your nails hard enough into your skin and it could mimic what's happening in your dreams. So yes, it's quite possible you guys are hurting yourselves and it could all be affected simply by waves in the atmosphere."

Danny couldn't believe it. "You guys act like it's as simple as getting cranky during a full moon."

"Simple? I don't think I ever said anything was simple, but yes, people are affected by a ton of different things. Do you have any idea how many crimes are actually committed on the full moon? The cycles of the moon can affect people's moods, and why should this be any different? You guys are being influenced by something and if it has to do with something physical, we can work on that. And look, at the very least, we're out of the house and there's a good chance the tornado can't find you now. I think that thing is real and is simply some sort of magnetic reaction you're both materializing."

Danny's eyes were wide. "You think we're conjuring it up ourselves?"

"It's possible. Bring enough energy together and who knows what can happen? You and Katie have powers that channel energy, so why not? Mom and Dad told me it seems to be settled on either the house or Magnolia Fields. Maybe there's something in both those places magnifying your abilities."

Danny stared at him. "We're not making the mass up. It's an evil thing attacking us."

Michael pursed his lips. "I don't know what that thing is. But, if it does have something to do with electromagnetism and the earth, maybe it's something you're creating. If you're not, it's new and something we've never seen before."

Danny huffed. "Wow. I'm a superhero who can create a tornado of death that can move on the ground and follow people. Who knew?"

Michael snorted. "Look, what if there is something buried somewhere that was suddenly activated—helping this thing manifest? If it draws energy to itself, maybe it is creating this tornado and following you, because it is somehow drawn to you and Katie? That's not so farfetched. Did Mom and Dad discuss this idea with you yet?"

Danny shook his head. "No, they didn't." Though it did made sense. He did think something was working on his sister and him in those two places and causing the disturbances.

"Well, I think that's what it is, too. Don't worry. They're smart. They'll figure it out, and we'll be safe at the lab."

Danny wanted very much to believe him.

They turned off the exit and rode a mile through barren farmland. The moon was bright and the light reflected off the snow on the fields, making it haunted and eerie. Danny shivered. For a moment, he flashed back to a scene when he and Michael were on the run for their lives so many years ago. He remembered a harrowing car chase through side roads, running from the cops and Herrington's people, and barreling through the woods with only the moonlight as their guide. There had been a moment their car had nearly overturned and he remembered the feeling as his stomach lurched and he'd been thrown against the inside wall of the vehicle. But they had gotten away. Maybe their luck would hold up a little longer.

Michael turned onto a side road, passed a crumbling rock wall and then into a complex designed to appear abandoned. They navigated through a series of deserted cottages, which had been left to nature, but he knew it had been done intentionally for privacy purposes. Basically, the entire first leg of the entrance to the facility was a virtual ghost town. But, over three thousand people worked in the facility on any given day, though now it was eerily quiet. They didn't pass any cars coming from the opposite direction.

"That building over there always creeps me out," Danny signed. He pointed at a crumbling structure, complete with collapsed concrete walls and broken windows. The shutters were hanging sideways or were missing altogether. The outside wall was stained with black streaks, the paint long gone. Danny swore it always reminded him of blood leaking from the empty windows like tears every time he saw it. He shivered as Michael drove by. Another turn led them past a broken greenhouse and an abandoned horse barn, but soon newer buildings sprang up. The dirt road gave way to smooth blacktop and after a few more winding turns Michael finally came up to a stone gatehouse. He pulled up and rolled down the window, smiling at the elderly man with the white goatee who was leaning his head out of the vestibule. "Hey Harry, how you doing this evening?"

Harry nodded, his usual craggy smile subdued for the evening. Harry had been a guard at the facility for over thirty-five years, and he was as much a fixture at the lab as the bronze statue of Stephen Hawkins in front of the main building. "I'm doing fine, son. You best get moving along. Your parents are already inside. Most folks took off for the weekend to beat the storm, so it's going to be pretty quiet around here for the next few days. I suggest you stay inside where it's safe." He leaned down and peered into the car.

"How you doing tonight, Danny? Your birds doing okay? Talking to you at all this evening?"

"I'm doing good," Danny spoke, giving Harry a thumbs up. Something was weird. Why was he asking him about his birds? He never did that.

Michael apparently didn't feel anything was out of the ordinary. "Okay, Harry. You have a good night and call us if you need anything."

"I would, son, but the phones are out, too." He paused and Danny swore he wanted to say more, but all he finally said was, "You boys be safe and take care of your family, especially that little sister you got there. She's special." He opened the steel gate. Michael drove through and then watched as the gate swung shut through the rear view mirror.

"That was really weird, don't you think?" Danny asked Michael.

"Why do you say that?" Michael asked as Danny turned around in the seat to stare behind him. Harry had moved out of the vestibule and stood in the road, watching them go.

"Something's wrong. He didn't joke with us like he normally does. Wasn't it strange the way he asked me about the birds and kept talking about us needing to be safe? He doesn't even know about my birds, does he? And that crack about Katie being special? I mean, how could he possibly know anything about her either?"

The snow started falling hard. Michael craned his neck forwards to glance at the sky. "Oh, he doesn't know anything about you or Katie. He was just making small talk and telling you to be a good big brother, that's all. And I heard he lives pretty far from here and with the impending storm, maybe he's just worried about getting home later tonight. Or maybe he just wants us to know not a lot of people will be on premises for a few days and with the phones not working, we'll just have to manage on our own, especially since he already saw

Mom, Dad, and Katie come in. Geez, Birdman, you really are on edge. Stop looking into everything. You're starting to make even me nervous."

The car veered around a bend and Danny turned around and sat back on his seat, facing forwards, but he still didn't feel right.

They drove through the winding roads, passed quaint Tudor-like buildings with bright trim. They were architecturally designed to resemble the homes in a small European village, but were really high-tech lab facilities. Trees lined the streets and ornate lampposts decorated the sidewalks that were bordered with now dormant flower gardens. Baroque streetlamp posts spewed a yellow light showing road signs with witty street names like Einstein Ave, Kepler Court, and Newton's Walk. In the back of the complex were the boarding houses for the staff and custodial help when they stayed overnight. Michael pulled onto Darwin Drive and parked in the back of a *cul-de-sac* next to a small, detached ranch house.

From Danny's vantage point, he could see the living room, the kitchen beyond it and to the left, a hallway that he knew led to two small bedrooms. It would be cramped, but at least they would have heat and electricity. And maybe they'd even be able to raid the kitchen at the facility in the morning. Danny's stomach rumbled as he recalled the amazing breakfasts the chefs made there over the years. He hoped they were working tomorrow morning.

As his brother parked the car, Maddy stuck her head out of the front door. A warm, inviting yellow light beckoned to them and spilled onto the front walk. "Oh, I'm so glad you're finally here. It took you longer than we thought it would. Why didn't you pick up your cell phone, Michael? I've been calling and texting you this entire time until I finally ran out of battery."

Michael glanced at his phone in surprise. "I'm sorry, Mom. It's dead. I must have forgotten to charge it." He smacked his head. "And, of course I left my charger back at the house."

Maddy shook her head and stared at Danny. "And you? I pay all this money for a phone and you probably have it sitting on your dresser, huh?"

Danny cringed, remembering exactly where he'd left his phone in his room. He had been about to get it, but got sidetracked helping Charity get her bags into the car. Great, now he wouldn't be able to even text his friends or play any games on it while he was stuck with his family. "I'm sorry, Mom."

She shook her head. "Well, it is what it is, isn't it? My charger is suddenly missing as well. We'll all just have to make due. Now come in already. It's cold out here." She glanced at the sky. "And the storm's coming in fast, too." She hustled them inside and shut the door.

It was warm and cozy and the bungalow smelled like cookies. His dad threw a log onto the fire and he could see sparks flying. Katie bounced out of the kitchen, her face dotted with smears of melted chocolate. Her grin stretched from ear to ear. Even her teeth were covered in chocolate. For the first time in days Danny relaxed, if even for a moment.

"Come on, Danny. Mommy has more in the kitchen," Katie signed.

With that, Danny threw his backpack onto the floor and followed his nose and his skipping sister back into the kitchen.

Chapter Fourteen

A gun was trained on Harry. The guard remained stock still, watching Michael and Danny drive off. His own weapon lay at his feet where he had thrown it. The snow was quickly covering it.

"That's a good man, Harry. You played that very well. I thought you might have messed it up at one point and I'd have had to take you out, but you got yourself under control. Now, nice and easy. Start walking."

Harry stared at the gunman. "Please, you don't have to do this. You don't know what you're getting involved in. Maybe I can help you."

"I know exactly what I'm getting involved in, Harry. I've known for a long time. And no, you can't help me. No one can. Now let's go."

"I know who you are." His voice was soft and he didn't move.

"Oh, you do?"

Harry nodded. "You look just like her, you know."

"Shut up. Don't say another word."

Harry smiled sadly. "You won't get away with this. Danny will stop you."

The gunman glared at him. "Danny won't be able to do anything. He doesn't even know what's going on. Now start moving or I swear I'll shoot you right here."

Together they trekked deep into the woods and minutes later a gunshot rang out. A lone dove took to the sky in a furious race to get away. It streaked straight towards the

Andersons. Another gunshot sounded and the dove, fatally hit, plummeted to the ground.

At that same moment, Danny glanced up from where he was sitting on the floor of the bungalow. He gazed through the window and to the sky as if searching for something. For a second he squinted and a frown passed across his features, but then his eyes cleared and he turned back to the television in front of him. The moment passed and he stuffed another chocolate chip cookie into his mouth.

It took only minutes to find the dove. It was dead and a quick glance into the woods proved it. A lone soul bobbed and floated within the trees. He was a mere shadow, with no chance now to move on to the light.

"Sorry, Harry. It had to be this way. Couldn't have you telling the Andersons what I'm up to yet, could I? Or, who I am." The gunman took out a small device from an inside pocket and clicked a button. A high keening noise pierced the night. Creatures rose up from the ground and through the snow, surrounding the bird. In a tumultuous, gluttonous feeding frenzy they attacked it. It was gone within minutes. A quick glance towards the woods and the shadowy form folded into itself and melted back into the trees.

It was a quick hike back to the guardhouse. Across the street was a small gardening shed with a motorcycle resting against it. For a moment the thought to use it to get closer to the Andersons was considered, but with the silence at the facility, the noise would be heard by the family. It wasn't worth the risk. So many precautions had been considered for every scenario. Painful staking out of the facility in every free moment, learning the schedules of each of the guards, sneaking in through the woods and setting up the equipment. It had been tough, and sleep had been hard to come by, but it would all be worth it in the end.

So when the lights and electricity went out in the Andersons' home, it wasn't a stretch of the imagination to know where the Andersons would go. To the bungalows, of course.

Herrington's assistant snickered and wondered how the infallible Gary Anderson would feel knowing someone manually shut off the heat and electricity on their block's grid. It hadn't been a mishap from the storm. The electricity was probably already back on.

The assistant put on goggles and attached snow shoes to their boots. A covered woodpile sat next to the shed and a quick pull of the tarp revealed a sled. Uncovering another layer of tarp exposed a box, with the machine lying snugly inside. The box went into the sled along with the machine and a large backpack with the rest of the supplies.

It took only minutes to wrap the tarp over everything to protect it from the falling snow and start the journey towards the Andersons.

The falling flakes made everything so tranquil and quiet and it gave the assistant a chance to reflect on things. Wondering about the task at hand and wondering how it was going to all turn out. So much of the planning over the years had been accomplished alone, with no help save hidden conversations with Herrington. But that was okay. The assistant was used to doing things alone and had basically been alone since childhood.

The assistant skied through the facility, dragging the sled past a quaint park called Faraday Fields and then passed the now empty Galilei's Gardens. No one could be seen in the empty streets. It was like being a ghost in a ghost town with no one to haunt.

Passing another guard post, a shadow bobbed inside it, just hovering as if it were still on duty. The assistant ignored the pair of bloody boots that stuck out of the door of the little building. A dead bird lay by the feet.

Of course, Harry hadn't been the only casualty that night. Without another glance, the gunman moved on.

Within thirty minutes, the illumination of firelight could be seen flicking through the windows of the Andersons' bungalow. With the partially opened curtains, it was easy to discern Danny and Katie watching television in the front room and Maddy moving around in the kitchen in the back of the house. Michael and Gary weren't in view and were most likely in one of the back bedrooms. Both cars were in the driveway and no fresh tracks had been made in the snow since the storm had started, so no one had left the house.

The gunman skied onto Pasteur Place and chose a house across the street whose front windows faced directly towards the Andersons' living room. Taking out a set of locking picks, it was only a few quick attempts to get inside. The snow was falling fast and soon the tracks from the sled would disappear.

Setting up in the living room, the lights off and the curtains partially closed, the assistant could move around in relative obscurity, all the while being able to see everything happening at the target.

The cellphone vibrated. "Yes?"

Sets of clicks sounded. Ah, Herrington couldn't talk, so he was sending a message in Morse code, clicking the button candies in the tin of mints.

A quick series of clicks back and Herrington was updated. As the gunman removed a wool cap, a cascade of blond curls escaped. Curls so thick and tight one knew if you tried to pull on them and then let them go, they'd spring back around her head like a jack-in-the box. Hair as curly as her father's and as blond as her mother's. Bright blue eyes gazed towards the machine.

Charity unpacked the unit and placed it on the couch. With a quick flick of the first dial, she turned back to the Andersons' window and watched. Katie put her hand absentmindedly to her forehead and rubbed her temple. Charity flicked on dial number two and Katie sat up, wincing. She turned on the third dial and Katie cried out. Danny also flinched and ran to her side. He stared around and brushed at things in the air. Dispassionately, Charity watched the family come from all ends of the house and huddle together in the living room. Danny was signing frantically about someone following them, about the mass coming, and about someone experimenting on Katie when they didn't know it. He was being dismissed by his parents. She could see Gary telling Danny not to worry and that they were safe at the facility. These people were so stupid. No one gave Danny enough credit. He, more than anyone, knew what was really going on.

Charity smiled one of her rare smiles of satisfaction and flicked off the dials.

Tonight was it. Tonight she would go after the little girl.

She closed her eyes and concentrated. A slight ripple in the air rushed from her and spread throughout the living room. A lone spider braved the cold and crept out from the floorboards, scuttling to her and responding to her silent call. She bent down and picked it up in her palm, putting her face close to it. "If you can, send her a message. Tell her I'm coming soon."

She placed the spider back on the floor and it scurried away and disappeared behind the couch.

A light flickered in the dark behind her and she turned around, realizing the first dial of the machine was on again. Of course, that was her own fault. She had caused it by using her own powers and calling the spider. She glanced out the window and saw Katie holding her head again. The second light popped on and when Charity glanced back at Katie, she could see her laughing. Obviously, Katie had turned on the second light to get rid of her headache, all by herself. It had become as easy as breathing. But Charity didn't want her going up the dials yet.

"Oh, no you don't, Katie. Not until I'm ready for you." Leaning over, Charity flicked off the dials and shut the machine down with a special failsafe switch so neither she nor Katie could turn it on again. "We're both going to have to be careful, aren't we?" She knew she'd have to curb her own abilities and sit along for the ride until she could intervene. She sat back on the couch and thought about a conversation with Herrington only a month before…

Herrington's voice was a whisper so he wouldn't be heard by the guards. "You understand you're going to have to be the one to fight Danny when you're there."

She had realized that. Who else had the power to do what had to be done?

"How much are you practicing?" Herrington said.

"Every single day, Father."

"Good. At least thirty minutes, each day. Have the headaches disappeared yet?"

"Yes, they left nearly a year ago. If I push too hard I'll get a nosebleed, but that's the worst of it. I understand the same thing happens to Danny."

"What level are you up to?"

"I'm already at level thirteen."

She heard the sharp intake of his breath. "You need to be at fifteen."

"I know. I'm trying."

"Trying? If you don't get to level fifteen, then you won't be able to stop Danny when he comes to help his sister. His

powers will be stronger than yours and you won't be able to do anything. I needed you further along, Charity." Even whispering, she could hear the acidic tone of his voice.

She held her tongue, a biting retort threatening to move past her lips. She counted to ten before she spoke again.

"Father, I'll be ready. It's not like I haven't been busy. I've been training, monitoring the Andersons and the lab with any free moment I have, and going to grad school. Not to mention making sure Michael falls in love with me. It's not just me that has to be at level fifteen, but Katie, too. Once she's there, Mother can make the jump, but only then. I've worked too hard on this and dedicated my life for too long for it to go wrong by rushing. And Danny will be strong, but he won't understand what's happening. If we're quick, we can leave both of them there before they even figure out what we're doing. And I've had to do this mostly by myself."

Herrington was silent for a few moments and then Charity heard the faint click as he severed the phone call.

He was obviously angry, but she understood. Stuck in a cell with no control and no real way to help her except for her visits to the jail as one of his lawyers or as a visiting psychologist or nurse in the infirmary. A few drops of a modified toxin on his dinner tray and a raging fever would overtake him, making him spend a few days in the sickbay. Both of them knew it would go away in days, but it gave them time to speak. She understood his frustration and his anger.

She was upset, too. Who did she have to turn to for help outside of her father? One of his rogue scientists? Creeping around the globe to find those who still worked outside the law, still loyal to Herrington, but too cowardly to do more than offer her the simplest of aid? None of them was ever allowed to know the true reason for her research. Herrington had been adamant about that. Soon that would all change. Once she had her mother by her side, they'd devise a plan to get her father out of jail and pay back everyone for what they'd done to her family. Especially the Andersons. She looked forward to getting rid of Danny. He was the reason her mother was dead and her father in jail. Maybe if her father hadn't been sent away, he could have saved her mother. Maybe if he hadn't been sent away, Charity could have come home from school and had the chance to say goodbye to her before she died, but instead she'd had to hide so the FBI wouldn't find out about her. Her parents had kept her their biggest secret.

She would have to remember to give her father better news the next time to mollify him. Until then, she would work on getting herself up as far as she could, because just like Katie, she too had the ability to speak to insects, to feel electromagnetic charges, and to manipulate them. She had always had an interest in her parent's studies and once she found her father's plans to modify the Andersons' version of the machine, she had set to work creating the ultimate version and using it on herself. Using pointers from her father and information from random scientists still loyal to him, she had honed her own skills, working alone until she could see below. The mass didn't bother her. In fact, it beckoned to her and that's how she knew she was connected to it somehow. It was how she knew that it was partially linked to her mother. Every level she achieved brought her closer to her mother and soon she would be able to help her make the switch and join her in this reality.

She remembered Herrington saying Katie's, Danny's, and her abilities were possibly reachable by hundreds, if not thousands of others around the globe. Just like people who were telepathic, who seemed to have a sixth sense about things, it simply meant they could tap into certain areas of their brains others couldn't. It was the same with the electromagnetic waves. If you trained diligently and persevered, possibly anyone could learn to do what Charity was quickly mastering.

Charity thought back to another conversation with her father.

"Why do we need Katie in the first place? I mean, when I'm able to get to level fifteen can't I just bring a suitable host to mom?"

"Maybe in the future, Charity, but not yet. We need someone with the innate ability to travel to that realm with you. The beings must be drawn to them. Katie feels these things from below and Marta will be able to seek her out like a beacon of light and rise from wherever she is. It's like with Danny. The birds can feel him and their souls seek him out. It will be the same with Marta. Her soul will feel for her and understand. Another person won't have that element we need, and furthermore, what if you bring along a host that fights you? How will you compensate?"

"I understand. So taking Katie is two-fold. She's young and she's that beacon of the power Mom will be searching for."

"Yes," Herrington said. "But we'll only use her for a little while. Again, Marta can't remain in her body, because of the "cause of consciousness." No two souls can exist in the same body simultaneously for long. One or the other will eventually go insane. She can simply attach herself for a little while. But there won't be time for second chances. We must make this work the very first time we try."

They were nearly there. Last night's training had been simply amazing. Katie was already at level twelve in such a short amount of time, and it was all Charity's doing. Herrington had no idea how incredible his daughter really was, but he would learn as soon as she succeeded and as soon as she got him out of prison. Then maybe she'd get the credit she deserved, and so desperately craved, from him.

Charity closed her eyes. Soon her life would be back on track. She'd have her mother by her side and everything would finally be better. Better than the past seven years, that's for sure. She glanced back at the window and saw Danny sitting again on the floor with his sister with his necklace firmly around his neck. Excellent. The dampening field was activated. Her little gift was disruptive to Danny's ability to call his birds. The links of the chain were a combination of elements that obstructed the waves from penetrating. Even the concentric circles around the pendant were an added barrier and she had laughed inwardly when Michael had complained to Danny about not wearing her gift. So, Gary must have taped it together yet again and now it was back around his neck. If he had it on as well at the showdown, all the better, unless she was able to get rid of him beforehand. It all came down to how far along his sister was and if she was going to still need him to move Katie along.

Charity dragged one of the reclining chairs towards the front of the living room where she could observe the family in relative comfort and possibly grab a few hours of sleep before she made her move. She closed her eyes and her memories returned to when she was a little girl, on her way to boarding school. It had been one of the defining moments in her life and one that had shaped her psyche profoundly. She was strong because of what she had endured and hardened from certain emotions caused by it. It had taken her years to understand, but she knew now why her father had sent her away. Besides keeping her a secret so she would be safe from the hands of his enemies, he also hadn't wanted a weak, meek little girl for a daughter. He had probably been disappointed in the first place she hadn't been a boy. Except for her mother, he looked down on most women, believing they were pathetic, sniveling creatures. Herrington expected none of those traits from his own child. He demanded someone intelligent, independent, and strong.

She had tried so hard to please her father and remembered how brave she'd been on the day they had sent her away. How she had promised herself she would never cry in front of her dad. And she hadn't. It was as if she had stuffed that emotion far away in her psyche, so far down she couldn't get to it even if she wanted to. Even now, she never cried.

The snow continued to fall outside the window, like tufts of cotton floating from the sky.

And her mind floated away, back to the past…

The little girl stood stoically on the platform, the nanny at her side gripping her bare hands with her white gloved ones. Nanny Prim, an English governess who had been in their service since her birth, accompanied her on this trip and she'd been told repeatedly she was not to cry or her nanny would box her ears if she did. Her father wouldn't approve of it and she had to be brave. That if she stayed strong, her father would love her more, and she so desperately wanted his love.

The little girl clutched an elegant porcelain doll to her chest. A dainty white pocketbook with a wallet, some photos and other knickknacks draped her thin shoulders. Mink fur trimmed her cream-colored winter hat and coat and her white patent leather shoes glowed brightly from a fresh polish. The little girl's bottom lip trembled slightly as she stared at her parents, but she listened to Nanny Prim and kept her emotions in check. Her father really did hate tears and she didn't want to disappoint him.

Samuel and Marta Herrington came up beside them with the rest of the little girl's luggage and gave it to the porter to place in her cabin on the train. "You're not crying, are you,

Charity?" Samuel looked down upon her, his eyes squinting judgmentally.

"No, Father," she replied, craning her head up to look at him. She swiped savagely at her eyes. "Just blinking from the cold."

He pursed his lips, reproachfully. "Good. You're six-years old and too big to act like a mewling infant. Listen to Nanny Prim, who will accompany you to school and introduce you to Headmistress Matilda Dewhurst. They're expecting you." He leaned down and patted his daughter on the head, the most affection he would offer. "Good luck, and make us proud." He turned to his wife. "Marta?"

Marta bent to the little girl's level and smiled. Her expression was a mix of emotions. She'd never been motherly and was uncomfortable showing sentiment to her only child. She raised her hand and was about to pat Charity's cheek, but froze mid-air. The awkwardness between them was palpable.

Charity uttered a small cry and pushed herself into her mother's arms, hugging her fiercely. Marta stood there for a moment, her arms out, unsure. With a bit of effort, she wrapped her arms around her, gave her a hug and then pushed her back at arm's length. Marta patted her head and pushed a wayward blond curl, which had escaped from her cap, back underneath and behind her ears.

Adjusting her scarf until she was satisfied, she stared into Charity's eyes. "You'll do great things there, Charity. It's the best boarding school in the world with the most rigorous academic program around. Presidents and scholars come out of there, people of great importance in the world. You'll be living with the sons of kings and queens and the children of heads of state. So, make us proud. We'll visit you on break in just two months' time." Marta straightened and moved next to Herrington.

Charity stared at her mother and bit her lip. Nanny Prim shook her shoulder to prompt her to answer and Charity quickly nodded her head. "Okay, Mommy."

And with that, six-year-old Charity turned her back on her parents and walked onto the train with Nanny Prim to take the first leg on a long journey across the sea. They had arrived at the airport, then made their way on a transatlantic flight to Switzerland where she had been schooled and groomed until she graduated. Samuel Herrington had picked the finest, most expensive private academy in the world, researching ruthlessly to find the one best geared to his daughter's superb intellectual abilities. He knew how smart she was because from a very young age he'd subjected her to rigorous intellectual and emotional testing to determine her capabilities. Her IQ was at the genius level, just like his and Marta's, but that was no surprise to him. Her capabilities would, of course, be great and besides the expensive tuition, he personally donated half a million dollars each a year to the academy, guaranteeing they had the top-of-the-line electronics and academics and his daughter was guaranteed the most attention she could get.

Charity's parents visited twice a year, staying for a week at a time. For two months during the summer she would return home. Sometimes she would go to California, but most times it was to wherever her father and mother had conducted their most recent scientific endeavors. Each winter and spring break they would take her on vacation with them, touring through Europe, enjoying symphonies, operas, and skiing in the Alps. They'd eat at the most decadent of restaurants and visit wonderful museums. She remembered her favorite trip to Rome when she was fifteen, peering up at the ceilings of the cathedrals, her father schooling her in the history of one religion or another. He was always teaching and training her. Religion intrigued him, but it was the afterlife that occupied his thoughts most of the time. He wanted his daughter to be a thinker, but to have it based on scientific knowledge and facts, not simple fanatical beliefs. He despised those who led their existence, and determined how they acted, based on the concept of blind faith in tomes created by men thousands of years ago. It made no sense to him and so he wanted Charity to question everything and to have her decisions based on logical theories. Everything he did, or explained, was to make Charity her very best, because he expected nothing less than perfection from his only child.

Her time with them was always limited. Breaks always seemed to end too quickly and she would return to Switzerland. So, she learned to do without her parents and to get from others what she lacked from her own family. She was a superb actress and discovered a pretty smile and a toss of her blond curls could get her farther at times than a solid pedigree and good grades. If she wanted attention, she would seek it. If she wanted solitude, she sought it out. She used her brains to get ahead and her looks to sway people her way. Like Michael Anderson. How easy he'd been. A quick smile, a blush, some light joking and fawning on his every word and he was putty in her hands. She had a way with boys and used her looks to manipulate them to do anything she wished. She remembered her conversation with her father only six months ago.

"Did you get into the graduate program in New York?"

"Of course, I did. I'll be starting in September."

"And you'll be in the same classes as Michael?"

"I'll make sure we overlap in at least one, but it's hard as we're in different years. The good news is our labs are connected in the same facility and I'll make sure we have ample opportunity to run into each other. I'll have him eating out of the palm of my hand in no time."

Herrington was quiet and gave her one of his rare compliments. "You remind me very much of your mother, Charity. Well done."

"Thank you, Father."

That was how Charity had ended up in New York University's graduate program and how she had met Michael on the corner outside of the biochemistry building. It hadn't been a random occurrence. Not by a long shot. And she was amazed at how easy it had been. She had flashed her smile, giggled at his silly little jokes, and had won him over in no time.

Such a fool. She wondered how he would feel when he found out she didn't care a wink for him. He would probably be terribly hurt. The boy was so ridiculously sensitive.

He wouldn't have lasted a minute with her father.

As her thoughts drifted further, she thought of her bugs and the places they had shown her, and fell into a light sleep.

Danny paced the living room and then leaned his forehead against the bay window, staring at the sky. He closed his eyes and tried to call for his birds, but nothing happened. He felt like a part of him had died.

Maddy placed a gentle hand on his shoulder to get his attention and he turned to her. "Danny, what's the matter?"

"My powers are gone again. I can't call to my birds."

"But you felt something just now in the living room when Katie's headaches started?"

He nodded and watched his father wave a device around the room, checking for magnetic and electric charges. "It's not reading anything much."

Danny shook his head. "It wasn't strong, but for a brief moment something charged the air and that's why Katie got a headache. And I can guarantee you this. It didn't come from her."

"Hey, I didn't do anything," Katie said, piping up.

"No, you didn't at first, but you did right afterwards, didn't you? First you got a headache and then you made a little rustle in the air and your headache disappeared, didn't it?"

Katie nodded and bit her lip.

Danny turned to everyone. "We're not alone. Something's here playing with us, right now. They're working on Katie and they're not going away. I can feel it." He turned back to the sky and called for his birds, but again, nothing happened. Something was very, very wrong.

He saw his dad tap Michael on the shoulder. "Come on. I want to make sure the windows and doors are secured and see if we can get anything together for weapons. " He and Michael moved around the bungalow.

Maddy called after them. "Gary, wait. You know what might work? If this thing has something to do with electromagnetic waves, could we somehow create a barrier against it?"

Gary stopped in his tracks, thinking. Finally he shook his head. "Maybe if we were all in a lead room, but remember, if we create something to block this thing out, Katie and Danny couldn't feasibly do anything either. They'd be blocked as well, right? If this thing is stronger than they are, they'll have no defense whatsoever. At the very least, if Katie's headaches are bad, she can stop them, right?"

Danny shook his head. "It won't matter either way, Dad. She doesn't know how to control them, yet, and I apparently can't do anything right now to help her." Danny was so frustrated he could have screamed.

His father nodded. "But your abilities may come back at some point. We don't know why they keep disappearing, so I'm not taking any chances. If this thing comes and we have no idea how to fight it, I'd rather you don't have a barrier working against you if your powers suddenly reappear." He faced his family. "I want everyone to think hard about this. What is this thing going to do? What does it want? Does anyone have any ideas? Any theories at all?"

No one had any and so he and Michael turned and moved through the house.

Danny watched them go, knowing what was coming for them didn't care about locks or doors or barriers. It traveled in the very air they breathed. Their phones were down and their contact with the outside world was shut off. Danny swallowed hard. No one had to tell him they were in serious trouble.

He turned again to the sky and sent out a message. He pushed so hard he thought his head would explode and nothing happened. He fingered the pendant on his necklace, rubbing it between his fingers absently, when his stomach flip-flopped as he remembered something. What did his dad just say? Something about creating a barrier, but if they create one his powers could also be blocked?

He frantically thought about when his abilities seemed to cease for the first time. It happened once when his sister was with him in his room when the mass attacked and Dr. Polensky had sacrificed himself. It even happened when they were fighting the bees. And even in his dreams the birds wouldn't listen to him all the time. He fingered the necklace again, staring at the metal links. Could it be? Every single time he had a problem he had been wearing the necklace. He started thinking furiously. Didn't Katie rip the necklace off of him in his room and then he was able to call the birds right after that? He had taken the necklace off in the basement when they worked with Katie on the machine and his powers had reappeared. It was the necklace. The gift Charity had given him. He ripped it off his body and ran to the window, fuming.

"What are you doing, Danny?" his mother signed.

He told her to wait a second and then sent out a rustle with his mind. He felt his powers start, but they were too weak to do anything. He threw the chain to the floor and tried again. The power flew from his body as if someone had taken an enormous weight off his chest and he could suddenly breathe again. Relief flooded his being. In seconds, a flock of birds streaked across the sky and moments later alighted on the front lawn. He leaned his face towards them and sent out a message his family was in trouble. That he might need help soon.

"We'll be here when you need us, Danny." With that, they took flight, leaving to find coverage from the storm.

Danny turned around and picked up the necklace, holding it out to his mother as if it were a venomous snake. "This is what's hampering my abilities."

Confused, Maddy took the necklace and held it up to the light. "Didn't Charity give this to you?"

"Yes, she did, and all my problems started then. I'm telling you, Mom, she's the one that's causing all this."

Maddy cocked her head, unconvinced, as Michael and Gary came back into the room. "Who's causing what?" Michael asked.

"Your girlfriend, that's who."

"What are you talking about?" Michael asked.

Danny took the chain out of his mom's hands and threw it at his brother and Michael flinched, catching it one-handed as it hit his chest. "She got me this and you know what? I can't do anything when I'm wearing it. And if you weren't so gaga in love with this chick, you would have realized that."

Maddy tried to calm him down. "Danny, please. Why would Charity do anything to hurt you? For goodness sake, it was simply a gift. It's only a necklace,"

Katie walked over to Michael and took the necklace in her hand. "Yuck," she said, flinching and throwing the necklace to the floor. She put her hand to her mouth as if she'd been burned.

The family turned to her.

"That thing feels weird. I don't like it."

Everyone just stared at the necklace lying on the carpet.

Michael shook his head. "No, it can't be true. It doesn't make any sense. I've known her for months and she's the sweetest, nicest girl I've ever met. I mean, if she were going to do something to us, don't you think she would've been plying me for information from the very beginning? She's never asked me anything about you guys. In fact, she's the least intrusive girl I've ever met."

"Yeah, maybe that was part of her plan," Danny said, fuming.

Michael glared at him. "Listen to me, if Charity were involved in this somehow, why would she have let herself get stung by bees? Does that sound rational to you? She could have done something to us, not to herself. Why didn't you get attacked badly, or Mom and Dad? If she wanted to hurt someone, she had ample chances. She had Katie sleeping soundly next to her after we thought she had disappeared. If Charity wanted to do anything to you or Katie, she could have done it at any point she stayed with us. You're wrong about her."

Danny peppered him with questions. "What do you even know about her? I mean, where is she really from? And don't you think it's weird she studies bugs? I mean, what girl studies stuff like that?"

"Danny, stop it. That's the stupidest thing I ever heard. You're not convincing me Charity has any part in what's going on right now. You saw me put her back on the train myself," Michael yelled, balling his hands into fists.

"Calm down, Michael," Maddy said. "We have to figure this out."

He shook his head and picked up the necklace, letting the metal strands run through his fingers. "It doesn't make any sense. It's just a necklace."

Danny walked over to him and put his hand forcibly on his shoulder, making him look at him. "Did you actually see her get on the train, Michael? You left her at the depot and said your goodbyes there. She could have gotten off the train."

Michael pushed him aside, angrily. "And then what? She hitchhiked here, in the middle of nowhere in a snowstorm so she could do more crazy things to us? Why, Danny? What's the incentive? You still haven't given me one good reason why Charity would do this. And for that matter, her parents live in Seattle. She's got one older brother who's a doctor and married with two little kids and a younger sister who studies acting in California. Anything else you want to know about her?"

"Yeah, there's a lot I want to know about her, not just the things she probably lied to you about," Danny said. "She could have told you anything and you would've believed her. I don't think the girl said anything you didn't slobber over the entire time she was here."

Michael's face turned beet red in anger and Gary put up his hand. "That's enough, Danny."

Danny shook his head and turned on his family. "No, it's not enough. I've been trying to tell all of you for the longest time what's happening and no one believed me. You keep denying what I say is real. That what's happening could be caused by solar activity or sunspot issues. It's not. It's her and she's the one causing all of it."

"But why?" Michael seethed. "What is her motive?"

Danny didn't say anything because he had no idea.

"You see, you have nothing." Michael stormed out the room and into one of the back bedrooms. Danny felt the vibration of the door as it slammed shut.

Gary stared at the direction Michael had gone and then turned to Danny, looking him squarely in the eye. "Do you know what she wants to do, Danny?"

Danny raised his eyebrows in disbelief. "You believe me?"

Gary glanced at Maddy who nodded and then he grabbed Danny in his arms and hugged him fiercely. He stepped back, signing. "I do believe you, and so does your mother. I'm so sorry we didn't listen to you sooner. But we're listening to you now. Tell us again your theories and I want you to start from the beginning from the first time you started having nightmares. I promise we'll have an open mind. As open as it gets."

Danny talked.

Chapter Fifteen

An hour later, Katie finally fell asleep in her parents' bed. Danny sat with his mom and dad at the kitchen table and watched them conduct tests on the necklace. Eventually, Michael came out of his bedroom and sat in a chair, sulking at the other end of the table. Danny knew he wasn't going to believe anything until he saw proof with his own eyes.

"Funny how your cell phone ran out of battery, isn't it?" Danny said to Michael. "Now that I think about it, didn't Charity use it up playing some dumb app game all morning? And come to think of it, didn't she also distract me when I was going upstairs to get my phone? Something about needing me to help her with her bags? I mean, all she had was one dopey little knapsack. Her pocketbook is bigger than that thing."

Michael glared him. "So tell me something, genius. What kind of superhuman powers does this girl have to get an invasion of bees to attack the house?"

"Katie can call bugs to her," Danny said. "Maybe Charity can, too."

Michael raised his eyebrows. "Oh, so now these abilities are rampant throughout society and you think Charity can do this as well? So she voluntarily got the bees to come and invade the house? Got them to attack her and give her over twenty stings? Yeah, that's what an evil maniac does. Makes sure they get themselves seriously hurt to take the attention off of what they're really doing, right?"

Danny squinted. "Maybe that's exactly what she did. If she has her own machine, she can call bugs and other stuff to her, too."

Michael slammed his hands on the table. "So now she also has her own machine? One that took Mom and Dad, scientists, years to make?"

Maddy turned to him. "Michael, calm down."

He stood, shaking and glaring at his brother. "No, I won't. He's accusing Charity of being some crazy killer and I want answers from him. So, where does she keep this so called machine, Danny? I've been with her constantly over the past few months, been in her dorm room, and I haven't seen anything. The machine isn't something you can just hide. And how in the heck does she have a machine anyway? It's not something you can just go and buy."

"Maybe Herrington helped her make it," Danny said, not backing down.

Gary glanced up from the necklace, taking the loop from his eye. "You think she's connected to Herrington? Maybe working with one of his rogue scientists? That's quite a leap."

Michael was dumbstruck and stared at his dad. "You're actually giving in to this? All of it?"

Gary nodded and put the loop back to his eye. "I'm sorry, Michael, but it's quite possible. It does fit together perfectly."

"Dad, it doesn't fit together at all. All of this can be explained. It could be a massive amount of coincidences."

Maddy flicked through a thick binder. She had been taking notes for the past hour. "That's not entirely true. All of this is just too similar to what happened to us seven years ago. When Danny initially asked us about Herrington possibly having made another machine, we disregarded it, but we shouldn't have. Katie is experiencing the same type of abilities Danny had when he was slowly moving up the dials as a child, but it's as if she's on a fast track. The question is how is she moving up so quickly? If someone else had a machine and was using it on her without our knowledge, then it would explain how these powers are coming on so quickly."

"And just when is Charity working on Katie?" Michael asked, incredulously. "She's in an intense graduate school program, practically lives in the lab and the other spare time she's been with me. And while at our house she stayed downstairs in the guest room."

"Were you with her at night? Did you slip out to see her at any point?" Danny asked.

Michael glared at him. "No, Birdman, I didn't. I stayed upstairs with you, because you're a scared little baby who can't sleep by himself, remember?"

Gary glanced at Danny and snapped his fingers. "Wait a second. Your nightmares. She could have been working with you and Katie while you're both asleep. That has to be it."

Danny nodded. "Syncing us up so we're together during our nightmares. And who is downstairs all by herself every night? Charity, that's who." He turned to Michael. "You're not with her when I have my nightmares. You weren't with her when the bees first attacked and you also weren't with her when Katie sleepwalked downstairs. She was alone each time."

Michael sat there, seemingly stunned.

Maddy nodded. "If there is another machine, it all makes sense, but this machine would have to have additional modifications to assist you both in syncing your mind waves for your shared dreaming."

Gary chimed in quickly. "Not to mention the electromagnetic and sound waves, too—this machine would have all of it. I didn't think it was even possible to create something so intricate and cross-platform, but with the right modifications you could build a device to work across different waves of the spectrum to make it as integrated as possible. Why not create a device that syncs them all? Of course, it would take years to develop and Charity is just a young girl. She would have had to have had help."

"I'll bet I know who that was," Danny said.

Maddy jutted her chin towards the necklace. "Gary, you see anything?"

He nodded and Michael sucked in his breath. "This isn't an ordinary necklace. It's made of a composite of magnetic and conductive materials. Look at the links." He held out the chain. "These aren't the conventional silver and gold links of standard chains. I think this is actually made out of sheet metal and copper."

Maddy raised her eyebrows, nodding. "Materials that can be used to create a superb dampening shield. Perfectly designed to completely impede Danny from having any of his own signals work when he's wearing or touching it. He couldn't call his birds to help him even if he wanted to."

Michael clenched his fists. "So you're saying it was all some big plan to meet me so I could bring her home and she could give you this necklace?"

Danny squinted at his brother. "I'll remember to ask her next time I see her."

Gary turned to Danny. "Stop it, Danny. This can't be easy on your brother." He returned to the necklace, eyeing it. "Even these concentric circles around the bird are questionable. It's like whoever designed this necklace was using Ampere's Law. With these radial segments, any arbitrary path would be hindered."

Danny sighed. "Dad, come on already. If you're going to get all scientific on me I'm not even going to look at you and try to understand what you're saying."

Gary eyed him. "It's really quite simple. Ampere's Law states that for any closed loop path, the sum of the length elements times the magnetic field in the direction of the length element is equal to the permeability times the electric current enclosed in the loop." He turned back to the necklace and looked at the wires under his loop again, as if what he had just said anyone could understand.

Danny simply stared at him and finally turned to his mom, but Michael answered instead. His face was ashen. "What Dad's trying to explain is the magnetic fields bouncing around inside the loops are stuck in those circles and can't get out. And now any electric currents flowing into them are affected. Though in your case, it's dampening your abilities. Those circles make that necklace basically a big, fat buffer."

Danny studied Michael for a moment before responding. "So you believe me now?"

His brother stared at him stonily for a few moments, when finally his shoulders drooped. "I don't know what I believe. But maybe."

"Whatever the case," Gary said, taking the loop from his eye and resting it on the table. "This necklace is staying outside for the night." He opened the window and laid the necklace on the sill and shut the window, locking it. Then he picked up the phone and put it to his ear. "Still dead."

Maddy bit her lip. "Maybe we should leave, Gary. We could try to get to the FBI home office. We'll be much better protected there."

Gary glanced out the window. "True, but the storm is getting worse and the drive will take us at least two hours, if not more. I think we'd be safer here than on the road. If Charity is around, I can't imagine she'll do anything tonight, all by herself in a storm. She's only one person."

"Like that's stopped her before? What about the charges, Dad?" Danny asked. "If she has a machine with her and she's around here, she can use it on us when we're sleeping. Then it won't matter if she's one person or a thousand."

Gary considered this. "We'll just have to weather one more night, Danny. Watch you guys like hawks and wake you up if you start doing anything in your sleep except smiling contentedly. In the morning, whether the snow stops or not, we'll get out of here and go straight to the FBI and get them involved. The last thing I want to do is get on the road in the middle of the night with no phones in a snowstorm and have to fight whatever it is that might be coming after us. It's better we're here sheltered from the elements and have a home base.

"Tomorrow I'll have the FBI do runs on Herrington to see if he has had any visitors recently and get an entire background check on Charity."

Maddy shook her head. "Daley will never believe it when we tell him what's going on."

Danny was fond of Bob Daley, the FBI agent who had tried so hard to help keep him and Michael safe seven years ago when they had been on the run for their lives. It seemed like no matter what he did, though, somehow Herrington was able to keep one step ahead of them. It was by sheer luck, and his brother's will to keep him safe, that they had survived.

Danny stared at Michael and suddenly felt sorry for him. He stood and walked over to him. His brother looked miserable.

"I'm sorry, Michael. I really am."

Michael pursed his lips and shook his head. "Yeah, right. You hated her from the very beginning." Without another word, he got up and stalked to the bedroom.

There wasn't much more to say. Gary rechecked the doors and windows, took a kitchen knife with him into his bedroom and the family went to bed for the night.

At three in the morning, Danny woke from a nightmare with Michael shaking him to wake up. He had been calling for his sister in Magnolia Fields, but he couldn't find her anywhere. Black shapes circled him, shoved him and blocked his way and no matter how hard he tried to move, they wouldn't let him out of their embrace to search for her. Finally, he had pushed through and then felt Michael grip his shoulder hard to come awake. He jumped out of bed and ran into his parents' room and woke them. They immediately turned to the couch against the wall where their daughter had been sleeping.

She was gone.

Chapter Sixteen

Danny and his family ran into the living room and froze when they saw the front door ajar. Cold air and snow drifted in.

Danny stared at them, exasperated. "You guys are impossible. How can you not hear her when she leaves?"

Maddy was stricken, unable to answer. She opened the front door further and peered outside. The storm was brutal, with the snow coming fast and furious. There was at least a foot of it on the ground. A pair of small footsteps led away from the house and the snow was quickly covering them.

"Her boots are gone," Michael said, staring at the pile of shoes on the floor next to the front door.

"So's her jacket," Danny added.

They threw on their clothes and trudged through the snow, calling for Katie. Her trail led them to the driveway, and they were met with a second pair of larger footsteps in the snow.

Danny pointed to the cars, his heart sinking. The tires on both were slashed.

Maddy grabbed Gary and pointed to where the footsteps continued. They moved across the street and towards the house across the *cul-da-sac* from theirs.

They pounded on the door. Gary pushed against it and when it wouldn't budge, together he and Michael kicked it down. They stormed into the house and into the living room while Maddy turned on the lights.

Michael groaned and fell to the floor when he saw the red scarf with the little ant designs lying on the carpet. He held it up to his parents, his face miserable. "It's Charity's. I got it for her birthday last month." He stood, his jaw clenched. "She's not going to get away with this."

They searched the entire house and checked all the rooms, the bedrooms, and closets. Charity and Katie were nowhere to be found.

Gary barked out orders. "I'm going to go out the back and start checking the other bungalows on the block and see if I can figure out where they went. Look for footsteps or any trail they left. If you find them, come get me immediately. Maddy, I want you to go to the picnic area and the lake and check those areas out. Danny and Michael, I want you both to stick together and get to the lab facility and see if they went there. Find someone who has a cell phone and call security and the local police. I want everyone back at the house to regroup in one hour. You hear me?" He grabbed Danny's shoulder. "What do you think she's trying to do? What does she want with Katie? We have to know so we can be prepared. Everyone, think. What is the link we're missing?"

"It must be Herrington," Maddy said.

"And what was the most important thing in the world to Herrington?" Gary asked.

Maddy's eyes widened. "Marta?"

"His wife," Gary said, snapping his fingers. "But what can Katie possibly do about Marta?

Danny chimed in. "She's evil, right? Maybe they're trying to get Katie to go down and find her."

"Down where, Danny?" Michael asked.

"Down to the level fifteen of that realm. Maybe that's where Marta is and it's why they're working with her to build up her powers so fast."

"What will happen when they get there? What would that do? Could they control her while she's there, Danny? And if so, do you have any idea what they would use her for?" Gary asked.

Danny shrugged his shoulders helplessly. "I just don't know, Dad. No one from level fifteen has ever been able to control me. I don't think that's it."

"Okay, then we'll just have to find out later. Everyone, get going," Gary said.

They left the house, separating in the driveway. With no footsteps to follow, Gary started moving to the house next door and Maddy trudged towards the lake.

Danny stood with Michael in the driveway. He was so frustrated. His sister and Charity couldn't simply vanish, but that's what they seemed to have done.

"Where do you think they went? Can you locate them?" Michael asked.

Danny closed his eyes and tried to feel for his sister, to sense any changes in the atmosphere, but couldn't sense anything except the snow pelting his face. He watched his father reach the next house on the block and break a window to get inside. His mother had already disappeared into the woods, which led to the picnic area by the lake. He didn't want to think of his sister down there and pushed the thought quickly aside.

Michael got his attention by grabbing his arm. "We need information. Can you call the birds to you? Maybe they can help."

Of course. Why hadn't he thought of that? He concentrated, and without the necklace hindering him, his thoughts flew from his mind with ease and out through the air, soaring to someone who would heed his call. For a moment, his thoughts drifted to that stupid necklace and how much time he had wasted. He became angry at himself. Maybe if he hadn't worn it or accepted Charity's gift they wouldn't be in this predicament. Maybe his sister wouldn't be missing. Maybe he could have done something sooner to stop all of it.

He felt his powers weaken and thrust those negative thoughts aside. They wouldn't help him. He had to find Katie and find out what Charity wanted. Because he knew it was something bad. He knew that even with his parents and Michael helping, he might still be the only person capable of stopping what was going to happen.

He felt a reply deep in his mind and saw a Canadian goose streak towards him, a brown and white blur whizzing through the snowy skies. It landed on the ground next to him. "I'm looking for my sister. Can you feel anything different happening in the atmosphere? Any changes in the air that don't feel right, because that's probably where she'll be."

Danny felt confusion flowing from the creature and took a step forward. "What is it?"

The bird flapped its wings and took off to the sky, flying towards the woods.

"What did it tell you?" Michael asked.

Danny shook his head. "He said he can't see her, but something is happening in the forest. Something strong and powerful and extremely bad is pulling at him. It's exactly what Dr. Polensky told me. There's this constant tug on your being when you're a bird, like when you want something really badly and the feeling of it stays with you all the time and you can't help thinking about it. This tug is the pull of the light, telling you it's there and you can move on if you wish. The bird says this particular lure drawing him now is different. It doesn't feel right or safe or any of the other things the attraction to the real light brings. And the pull isn't going up like it should be, but coming from the woods. That's where we have to go. I'm positive it's where Charity's taken her."

Michael glanced down the street, his father now out of shouting distance. He was a small black speck in the distance, moving to another house. Their mother was nowhere to be seen. He took a step towards his father, but Danny grabbed his shoulder and shook him hard.

"We don't have time to get them. We have to go right now. Come on." He stopped and thought of something. "Wait a second," He turned and ran as fast as he could through the snow, Michael pounding to keep pace with him.

Danny crossed the street and into the driveway of their bungalow, zipped around his parents' car and slogged through the snow to the backyard until he was outside the kitchen window. He brushed off the wet slush and ran his hands along the windowsill. What he was looking for wasn't there and his stomach clenched. It had to have fallen. He dropped to his knees and started digging frantically.

He glanced up when Michael bent down next to him and tapped his shoulder. "What are you looking for?"

"I need to find the necklace Charity gave me. Help me, please," he said, throwing snow by the handfuls to the side.

Together they dug and Danny finally saw a glint of metal peeking through. With relief he grabbed it and slipped it over his snowcap, but let it hang over his scarf so it was visible.

"What are you doing?" Michael asked, incredulously. "You can't wear that. It'll dampen your powers and then they won't work. You're the one who said so yourself."

"Trust me, I know what I'm doing. Charity doesn't understand I know what this thing does. If she's planning something and thinks I can't interfere with her, maybe we'll get the advantage. I can always take it off. I don't know why, but I think we might need it."

Michael shook his head and his breath steamed in the air. "Your call, Birdman." With that, they moved as fast as they could through the snow and into the woods.

The woodlands were dense with pine trees and fallen logs, and with the snow pelting them, the going was slow. After five minutes of trudging through the forest, Michael patted

Danny's shoulder and he turned to him. He brushed the snow off his brother's face. "Danny, how are we going to find her in here? We're in the Adirondack Mountain range. There's no end to this forest for miles around unless we head back to the lab and the bungalows. We could be walking in here forever and not find her."

Danny shook his head, frustrated. "We have to try. She's here, somewhere." A shiver ran up his spine. "I feel something."

Danny took off his gloves and held up his hands. He stood stock-still, closed his eyes, and concentrated, trying to feel something in the air. There it was again, the softest of charges rushing by him. Yes, he could sense it and see where it was emanating from. It was coming from deeper into the woods.

"Where is she?" Michael asked.

"I'm not sure. Let me try again." Danny closed his eyes and held out his hands and waited. For a full minute he stood that way, the biting cold eating into his fingers, and was about to give up when the charge came again. He stretched out his hand, as if reaching for it, searching for its exact direction, and through the trees he could literally see the ripples in the air. They were forming into something.

Michael saw it, too, his eyes widening with fear. "What is that?" He took a step back.

Danny stared at him, shocked. "You can see them?"

Michael nodded.

The ripples were getting larger and darker.

Danny gulped. Ahead of them in the trees, shapes were developing. Grotesque figures appeared, flitting in and out of the trunks as if playing a hideous game of hide and seek. "Katie's over there."

"Is Katie doing this? Is she creating those things?"

Danny nodded. "She is and from their size, I can tell she's moving up the dials fast." He turned to his brother. "We have to get past them, but Michael, if she's as high as I think she is, these things will sting when they touch you. The fact that you can see them and Mom can't means you do have some abilities she doesn't. Just be prepared when we meet them. They hurt."

"Can we fight them?"

Danny shook his head. "No, we can't. All we can do is endure it and push through. Come on." He moved forward, and sensing him, the ghostlike creatures made a beeline for them. Soon they were surrounded and Michael fell to his knees as an unforeseen creature kicked him from behind, throwing him forward into the snow. Danny watched as a wispy apparition, with a vaguely human form, then hit his brother in the head and shoved him into a low thicket of bushes. Michael grunted and pushed himself to his feet. He flailed at the air. Creatures surrounded him, flitting in and out of his legs and brushing against his body.

"Danny, can you call your birds to you? Can they fight against these things?" Michael signed, swinging at the creatures.

Danny felt a sharp pain in his arm and then a nip in his leg. He ignored the attacks. "I don't want to call them yet. I don't want Charity to know we're here. Just push through them, Michael."

Easier said than done, as the creatures whipped around him, smacking his face and pinching his skin. Danny grabbed his brother's hand and together they plowed through the creatures and trudged through the forest, following the trail where the ripples came from. The creatures grew in number with each advancing step, as if they were entering their very den, which they essentially were.

The ripples distorted the air, the way they do when air rises against hot pavement in the middle of a summer heat wave. The very air around them was charged and pulsating and Danny could feel the power coming at them.

"We're close. Just a little bit further." They struggled through and emerged into a small clearing. Katie lay on the ground motionless, a thin layer of snow already covering her. Danny watched Michael rush to her side, but something happened and with a yell his brother fell to the ground and grabbed his leg. Horrified, Danny saw blood start pouring from Michael's calf, and realized the vibrations he just had felt in his chest were made from a gunshot. The snow below his brother turned red with his blood.

He started to moved towards his brother, but Michael yelled at him to stop and pointed towards the other end of the clearing. Danny followed his gaze and froze as Charity walked out of the forest. Her gun was trained on him.

"I wouldn't take another step if I were you, Danny. As you can see, I'm a very good shot. I could have killed him, you know, but what fun would that have been?"

Danny glared at her. "Fun? You didn't kill him because you knew if he were a bird maybe he could have gotten help and stopped you."

Charity laughed. "He has no powers as a human and I doubt, even as a bird, he would have given me much of a problem. Of course, I'd then have to kill him as a bird, too, and with the storm, it might have given me pause for at least a second. Not like with Harry the gatekeeper. So sad how he tried so valiantly to fly to help you." Charity made a sorrowful, pouty face with her mouth.

"You killed Harry? Why would you do that?" Michael asked, grimacing. He held onto his leg and glanced towards his sister, who was still lying motionless.

She snorted. "I had to. I couldn't let him ruin everything I've been working towards all these years, could I? That man knew a lot more then he let on. There was no way he could stay alive."

Danny looked back at his brother. The red stain beneath him grew.

Charity tossed her curls, mocking him. "Oh, stop being such a baby, Danny. It's just a superficial leg wound. He's not going to die. At least not yet, anyway. I just wanted you to know who's in charge and to make sure you didn't get in my way. Otherwise, I will kill you, birds or not."

"But not until you get my sister up to her fullest power, right?" Danny asked.

"Smart boy," Charity said. "Which reminds me." With the gun still pointed at them, she took a device out of her pocket and pressed a button. Katie flinched, and a strong wave of current shook the air. Danny finally saw the black box behind Charity. Fourteen of the dials were lit.

"What are you going to do with her?" Danny asked. "Why do you want her?" He wanted to call his birds, but not yet. He had to learn more.

Charity stared at his throat, where the necklace lay, seemingly satisfied. "That's none of your business." She put the device back in her pocket and kept the gun trained on Michael as she sauntered over to him. She put one hand into her other pocket and brought out a set of handcuffs.

Michael glared at her. His face wore a mask of emotions mixing from hurt and confusion to a furious rage. "Why are you doing this? I cared about you."

She stared at him disdainfully. "Cared about me? You hardly even know me."

"I know enough. You don't have to do this."

Charity laughed. "I know I don't have to do this. I don't ever have to do anything I don't want to do. But this I want to. Now, don't move or I will shoot you, because I don't love or care about you, you insipid, ridiculous boy. Now, hands behind your back." She deftly cuffed him.

"You won't get away with this," Michael said, his eyes slits.

"I already have."

She turned to Danny who now had the necklace in his hands. He held it out to her. "Would you like your gift back?"

"Put it back on," she ordered him.

"Or what? You'll shoot me?"

"Maybe I should. You'll only get in the way."

Katie flinched again and must have made a noise, because Charity turned and glanced at the machine. All fifteen dials were lit.

She turned back to Danny, her smile pure evil. "Well, guess what? It's my lucky day. I guess I don't need you any longer at all now."

Danny dropped the necklace to the ground as Charity aimed the gun at his head.

A raven flew from the sky and slammed itself into the back of Charity's head. She fell forward into Danny. The gun flew from Charity's hands and Danny pounced on her.

"Here we go, Charity," he smiled, grabbing her wrists.

"Not so fast, Danny. You're all coming with me." Her eyes glinted.

They all fell unconscious to the ground.

The raven cawed to the sky and then grabbed the necklace lying on the ground.

A lone Canadian goose circled above their heads, honking at the four lifeless forms lying in the snow. It honked to the raven in reply and then whizzed down and plucked the necklace it clutched in its beak. And then, in a flurry of wings, it took flight, speeding across the sky towards the lake.

Chapter Seventeen

Danny woke lying in a pile of gray ash. The smell of sulfur was strong and it burned his nose and scorched his throat. He sat up, wiped his eyes and coughed ferociously. The air was acrid and each breath took a tremendous effort. He stared mutely at the landscape before him. From his vantage point on a small hill, he could see across the bleak horizon of a barren diseased land, filled with charred and burning trees as far as the eye could see. Cragged hills comprised of rocks and boulders punctuated the landscape and gaping crater-like pits dotted the terrain with dense plumes of smoke pouring from them. Rivers, coagulating with the bubbling blackness of oil streaked throughout the land, like scars, and he shuddered when he realized living beings floated within them, flailing as if trying to get out.

He glanced up at the sky, a blood red hue so dark it was nearly black and starless, but he could still see. It was as if he were standing on the moon, but one mutated to resemble someone's nightmares. He heard something and turned, glancing at the bottom of the hill. He was startled that he could hear. Ambiguous forms loped through the debris, stooped over as if bearing huge weights on their backs. Some resembled people, while others resembled nothing more than grotesque deformed animals, hunched down on all fours.

A hand touched his shoulder and he flinched. "Where are we?" It was Michael, his eyes wide with fear. Danny could see his brother's chest heaving in and out as he seemed to be trying to get his own breath back.

The ground shook under them. Michael threw himself at Danny and pushed him aside as the dirt split beneath them, revealing a gaping fissure. Vents of burning steam and lava shot up and Michael pulled Danny away from the burning ashes as they fell to the ground in smoking, smoldering heaps. One burning ember fell on his leg and Michael swiped it off.

"Thanks," Danny said.

"You're welcome." The brothers stared at each other and an unspoken message went between them. Danny realized he was no longer upset with Michael and he knew Michael again had his back. Whatever had happened before with them was over. Charity no longer had a hold on them. If her goal had been to split them up, she had failed.

"You can hear, here, but this isn't the level fifteen you took me to. Do you know where we are now?" Michael climbed shakily to his feet and then glanced at his leg. "My leg wound is gone. That's right. Our injuries don't follow us, do they?"

Danny shrugged. "I guess they don't. I think we're at level fifteen of the underworld. In a purgatory place, right before these beings have to move on, or down, or wherever they go."

"You took us here?" Michael asked, amazed. "I didn't know you could go down, too."

Danny shook his head. "I can't. Charity took us. When I tried to grab onto everyone's soul and take you to my level fifteen, I could feel Charity fighting me. She was using Katie as an anchor. There was a force about them pulling us and when Charity grabbed on to me, there was nothing I could do. She has powers, too, Michael, and they're really strong."

"So this place is the equivalent of your level fifteen in your bird world—before heaven?" He glanced at the blood red tableau above. "I don't see a gem or anything like that to move on to."

Danny shook his head, his face grim. "It wouldn't be up. Nothing in this realm is up. What we're looking for is down." He felt a violent tug deep in his being and spun around to see where it was coming from. Bile threatened to come up his throat. Below them was an enormous crater, as if a meteor had hit the land and shattered it. Thousands of moving, lurching figures surrounded the pit like a crowd gathering for a lynching. Dark apparitions resembling specters flew in and around it, shooting into the crater and then soared up into the sky. Danny stood and took a step forwards, feeling Michael at his side. Katie was down there.

"What are those things? Are they people?"

Danny nodded grimly. "Maybe in this land their fates are still being decided before they move on to whatever punishment they face. I'm not sure, but something is keeping these beings here. But Katie's down there with them. I can sense her."

Michael glanced around, pursing his lips. "Is Charity here, too? Can you feel her?"

He nodded. "Oh, she's here all right. I can feel her power pulsating all around us. It's like a bad rash, itching at my skin. I felt it the moment she touched my soul to bring us and now I can recognize her. Come on, let's find Katie and get out of here."

Michael grasped his arm. "What about our physical bodies in our reality? We're just lying in the snow, right? If we don't do something, we'll freeze to death."

Danny shrugged his shoulders. "There's nothing we can do about that. Since our body processes slow down when we're in that state, we should be okay for at least a little while." He hoped it was true, but what choice did they have? They had their winter gear on. It would have to be enough. Resolutely, he turned towards the pit and trudged down the hill. The ripples in the air were stronger over the opening and he moved in that direction. His heart pounded because he was terrified for his sister and what they'd find there. He wished he had a weapon, but he didn't think anything he could use would be strong enough to fight the battle he was sure was coming.

Chapter Eighteen

Maddy circled the lake, calling desperately for her daughter until her voice was hoarse. She took out a device from her pocket and tried to check for any electromagnetic readings in the area and found nothing. Frustrated, she began to make her way back to the bungalow, when a goose quacked overhead. It circled her and landed in the snow, next to where she was standing.

Maddy bent down to it, sensing it had come for her. "Do you know what's happening? Do you know where Katie is?" The bird hopped closer and Maddy noticed something hanging from its beak. She sucked in her breath when she recognized what it was.

The bird dropped the chain and Maddy scooped it up and put it in her pocket. "Please, take me to them."

Honking, the bird flapped its wings and took to the air, flying a ways and then setting itself down again as if in wait. Maddy understood and trudged towards it. The bird took flight again and she followed until she returned to the cottage. By the time she got there, she was sweating.

Gary came out of one of the houses, saw her and lumbered to her side. Wind and snow pelted their faces.

"She's not inside any of these houses. I can't find her anywhere," he said. "Did you find something at the lake?"

"This." She held up the necklace, breathing hard. "A bird found me and gave it to me."

She nodded towards the end of the block and Gary turned. A lone Canadian goose waited for them.

"Do we know who it is? Is it one of the…?" He couldn't finish the sentence.

"No, I don't know how I know this, but it's not Katie or one of the boys. But whoever it is knows where they are and will take us to them."

"Then let's go."

As if the bird understood, it took flight again and made towards the woods.

Maddy and Gary followed as fast as they could.

Chapter Nineteen

Danny and Michael made their way down the rocky slope. They sifted through dens of pure despair, filled to capacity with crippled creatures. These beings reached out to them with outstretched arms that were so thin their very bones seemed to glow from within. Without thinking, Michael reached towards one, but Danny pulled him back just seconds before the creature extended its taloned fingers, meaning to slice him in half. It spit and hissed when it realized it had lost its prey.

"Thanks, that was close," Michael said, swallowing hard. A crowd of dark shadows formed a wall in front of them. "How are we getting past them?"

Danny bit his lip. "I don't think we do." They had come to the bottom of the slope and moved towards the pit. The apparitions followed, swooped by them and turned their skin icy cold when they brushed by. Michael tried to push at them, but his hand went right through.

"Just keep going. I don't think the apparitions can hurt us here." Danny dodged one as it rushed past him. Another darted over his head and another swooped between his legs, but none stopped their progress.

"Maybe they can't, but I'll bet the people can." Michael's expression was grim as he tried to ignore the phantoms passing by him.

One flew directly at Danny's face. He flinched as the creature opened its mouth wide. Three sets of sharp, pointy teeth were ready to consume him. Danny closed his eyes and the ghoul passed over his face, leaving the stench of rotted meat to mix with the sulfur in the air. For a second his world exploded in the color red and pain, but then just as quickly it disappeared. He shook his head to clear it.

They stopped as they rounded a final bend. Their way was blocked by what Danny could only call monsters, but whom he knew were once people. Skeletal forms with translucent, shiny skin stretched over their bones. Their bodies were twisted and hunched in painful ways. The beings lurched and surrounded them. Danny was surprised at how strong they were when they grabbed their arms.

The boys tried to fight, but they couldn't stop the creatures and they were dragged over to the crater to hover at the edge like spectators at a game. Crowds of beings roared at the event.

Intense heat rose from below and Danny willed himself to lean over and look. At the bottom was his sister. Charity held onto her arms and dragged her over to an open fissure in the ground.

Katie's screams echoed across the pit. It excited the creatures and they let go of Danny and Michael as they hooted and hollered at the scene. The boys took the opportunity and jumped into the crater, sliding down the wall and crashing into those congregating at the bottom. Beings tried to swipe at them, but the boys pushed them aside and raced towards their sister.

Danny saw Charity glance up in surprise. With a glare, she wrapped Katie tightly in her arms, closed her eyes and an explosion rocked the air in front of him. Danny fell on his backside as a torrent of air charged in his direction, forcing him back. He climbed to his feet and tried to push himself against the barrier, but he couldn't get through. The ripples in the air were like an invisible force field and he couldn't run past it or force himself through it. He called out to his sister. "Katie, fight her. Use your powers." He could see his sister screaming and trying to yank herself away.

Michael threw himself against the field and Danny watched him blur into it, like a person moving into water, but the barrier stopped him as well and he popped back out.

"Michael, look!" Danny pointed towards Katie as the fissure next to her opened and widened. His stomach lurched as a white bony hand reached out to grip the dirt, like a dead person ripping their way out of a coffin and coming to the surface in a cemetery plot.

Danny closed his eyes and concentrated. He tried to take himself and his siblings directly to level fifteen, to counter what Charity was doing. He didn't even know if that was possible in this realm, but he pushed with all his might. He felt the power leap from his body, but to where it went, he didn't know. He felt Michael grab his arm and he opened his eyes. A blinding white light broke through the blood red sky, a single brilliant beam shooting out of it. It was just like in his dream. Danny concentrated harder—so hard his nose started bleeding and the bright slit grew and separated until it spread out like cracks of white spidery streaks breaking across the heavens. He pushed again, calling for help and he felt a reply. Birds flew out of the crack, making a bee-line towards him. Thousands came out, pouring like ants, whizzing through the sky and threw themselves into the ripples blocking them from Charity and Katie. Danny felt their pain as if it were his own as they hit the barrier.

Michael grabbed him and pushed him aside, throwing him to the ground as the ripples began to turn and twist, manifesting itself into the dark mass to fight the onslaught of the birds. It grew and expanded until it was hundreds of times bigger than them. It consumed the birds, throwing them out, their bodies nothing more than charred heaps growing into mounds. More birds heeded the call and finally a break in the ripples appeared before them, like the parting of a sea.

Without a second of hesitation, Danny and Michael slipped through the opening towards their sister.

Charity turned to them and scowled. Danny felt a charge emanate from her and an ogre-like creature with no eyes and a gaping mouth launched itself onto Michael. They fell to the ground, fighting.

Danny skirted around them and continued towards Charity. Beings grabbed at him, scratched him and tried to push him to the ground, but he dodged them. One reached out and grasped at his leg and he fell, sprawling into the ashy dirt.

He turned to the creature and tried to kick it aside. With a glance at the mass, he called out again for the birds to help him. One flew out of it and streaked towards him. It attacked the creature holding onto Danny and gouged its eyes. The creature shrieked and let go and Danny took that moment to get away. He turned and propelled himself towards his sister, who was now at the opening of the gap.

The hand from the fissure had pushed itself up and a head emerged. Thin wisps of blond hair clung to a sunken skull so hideous he wanted to look away, but couldn't. Katie shrieked and kicked at it. Charity pushed her towards it as the creature emerged from the hole and climbed over the crest. Danny could see it was a woman. A tattered yellowed dress hung from her gaunt frame and he could see sores bleeding freely on her exposed skin. The woman reached her bloody hands towards Katie.

Danny threw everything he had at the creature and it flinched. It turned to him when it felt his power. An ice blue gaze met him head on and he could see into her soul. His mind exploded in awareness and he realized without a doubt he stared at Marta Herrington. Now knew the connection. Charity was her daughter.

Marta smiled as she recognized him. Her mouth was filled with rotted teeth and a hideous black tongue. With a sneer, she turned and lunged towards Katie.

Danny flung himself forward, but Charity used her powers to send more creatures to stop him. They leaped onto Danny and forced him to his knees. He could see Michael still fighting desperately, but more creatures were attacking him as well. There were just too many of them and they couldn't fight them all.

He turned to his sister and watched helplessly as Marta grabbed Katie's hand. A terrible blackness sprung from their touch and Katie's body convulsed. Her eyes rolled back in her head and he felt his sister's pain and felt her revulsion in his very core. She screamed one final word before Marta pulled her towards the fissure. "Mommy!"

Marta laughed at Katie, the sound so hideous he felt like a knife had plunged into his gut.

He had to do something, but what?

They were trapped.

Chapter Twenty

Gary and Maddy followed the goose deep into the woods and when they got to the clearing, Maddy screamed in horror when she saw her children lying lifeless on the ground. She and Gary bent to them and brushed the snow off their faces and checked their pulses.

"They're freezing, but they're alive," Gary said.

"Oh, my God, Michael's bleeding." She fell to her knees and checked his wound. She saw the gun lying in the snow and her eyes widened. "Gary, he's been shot!" Taking her scarf off her neck, she wrapped it around his leg. "Where have they gone?"

Gary stared around, helpless. "Most likely to wherever Charity took Katie." He took off his jacket and draped it around his daughter. Then he laid his sweater on Danny.

Maddy stood up, her face a mask of anger. "We have to help them."

Gary stared at her. "How are we supposed to do that?"

Maddy stared at the scene and her mind suddenly cleared. She pulled the necklace out of her pocket and moved towards Charity.

"What are you thinking?" Gary asked. He cradled Katie in his arms and tried to warm her body up.

Maddy bit her lip. "I don't know. But I'm going to try something." She leaned down to Charity and placed the necklace around the girl's neck. "Maybe it will dampen her abilities."

"We could just kill her." Gary let that thought hang in the air.

Maddy and Gary stared at each other for a long moment, unspoken words flowing between them. Maddy finally shook her head. "I don't know if that will help them or not."

Gary held his lifeless daughter in his arms, rocking her like he did when she was a baby. "Then, I guess we can only wait." He leaned down and kissed her cheek.

Gary turned to Maddy to ask her a question and gasped.

She had fallen to the ground, unconscious.

Chapter Twenty-One

As Marta pulled Katie towards the opening, Charity suddenly grabbed her head and began screaming in anguish as if she'd been struck. She fell to her knees and the creatures, no longer under her powers, released Danny and Michael. The brothers ran to Katie when another ripple suddenly appeared in the putrid air in front of them. Maddy squeezed through it and fell to the ground with a violent thud. Disoriented, she blinked a few times before she glanced around and saw Katie being dragged into the fissure with Marta. With an inhuman roar, she lunged at her daughter and grabbed her leg before she fell inside.

When Marta realized something was holding Katie back, she glanced up and saw Maddy. An evil smile appeared on her face and she released her grip on the child, reached over and grasped Maddy's arm instead. Danny was horrified at seeing his mother suddenly appear, and then seconds later in Marta's clutches. He dove forward and grasped onto Katie and cast her to the side and safely away from Marta.

"Get Mom," Michael yelled, as he kicked at the demon attacking him.

Danny was already reaching for his mother. Maddy struggled against Marta and fell forward into the fissure. Lunging with everything he had, Danny pushed himself to the edge and grabbed his mother's ankle, gripping her left boot with both his hands before she disappeared completely. The blackness was as thick as oil and he couldn't see any part of her at all below her knees.

"Michael, help," he screamed. The strain of holding his mother pulled painfully at his shoulders.

Michael was instantly at his side and grabbed his legs. Danny heard him grunt. He glanced behind him to see Charity had recovered and had thrown herself on top of Michael, punching and kicking him to let go of Danny.

The pain in Danny's shoulders was intense as he tried to hold on. "Michael, I can't hold on much longer!"

Michael kept one hand on Danny and with the other he grabbed Charity's mane of curls and savagely yanked her off of him. She fell to the side and Michael viciously kicked her. She grunted and rolled away, but in seconds she was back. She threw herself onto Michael, pulling at his arms and tried to rip her nails into his face. He whirled around and punched her in her jaw and she fell to the side.

Danny could feel his grip on his mother's ankles loosening and called his birds desperately. A mass of them descended and flew straight into the fissure, disappearing into the black oil. In his mind, he heard a hideous shriek and the pressure on Maddy's legs ceased. He and Michael reached into the crevice and pulled their mother out. She was covered in a black gooey substance and was shaking uncontrollably.

Marta was gone.

Charity raced over to the edge of the fissure and screamed. "Mother! No!"

With an expression Danny had never seen before on his brother's face, even as they were fighting for their lives against Herrington so many years ago, Michael moved behind Charity and with both hands violently pushed her into the fissure. Danny could hear her screams echoing in his head as she vanished over the edge and disappeared into the black sludge.

A noise sounded behind them as other beings began to move towards them.

Michael turned to his brother. "Get us out of here right now." He motioned to Katie, who jumped into his arms and he grabbed onto Danny's shoulder.

Danny hugged his shaking mother to his chest and pushed his powers out to encircle his mom and siblings, felt deep into their souls, and latched on tight. Together, they soared up and out over the barren landscape towards the blood red sky, streaking straight towards the white beam. It was the only thing good in this land and it beckoned to him. He let his body answer and take the call. Together they flew into the light, Charity's screams dying away to nothing.

The world around them exploded in colors.

Chapter Twenty-Two

They appeared in a valley in the middle of a grassy field filled with wild flowers and rose bushes. Tall, majestic mountains reached to the blue sky and surrounded the dale. Their peaks were covered in snow and reached so high they disappeared into the white, puffy clouds floating above. The smell of honeysuckle and rose was strong and birds by the thousands streaked across the sky leaving rainbow trails in their wake.

Danny gripped his mother in his arms and he relaxed, letting her fall gently to the grass. She seemed dazed, but her shaking had ceased.

"Mom, are you okay?" He touched her face, but she didn't react. The black oil covering her had disappeared. What had she seen when she was in the fissure? What horrors had she endured?

"Mommy," Katie called to her and flew into her arms. Maddy focused on her and her eyes cleared. She glanced at Danny, then Michael and then around her. "I recognize this place. We're back in level fifteen in your bird world, aren't we?"

Danny nodded. "Yes, Mom. We're away from that horrible place."

Katie stared at him, amazed. "You can hear us?"

He nodded. "In these lands, I can." He turned to his brother who stared around him, silently. "Michael, are you all right?"

Michael turned to Danny, his eyes pained. "No, I'm not. I'm so sorry. I should have listened to you about Charity. This is all my fault. I'm such an idiot."

Danny shook his head. "It wasn't your fault. How could you know she was Samuel and Marta's daughter?"

A butterfly flew down and landed on Katie's outstretched hand and she gently pet its delicate antennae. The butterfly fluttered its wings a few times and then flew away.

Michael stared after it and then closed his eyes. "I thought she loved me. It was all just a lie to get to you and Katie. She just used me and I let her."

No one said anything, because there was nothing Michael said that wasn't true. He had been used and now he had to live with that knowledge for the rest of his life. Danny craned his head to look above him and saw the beautiful gem. It pulsed as if it were a living, breathing entity.

Maddy and Katie glanced up, too, and Katie jumped up and down, pointing to the sky, excitedly. "Oh. Can we go there?"

Danny shook his head. "No, that place isn't for us. We have to go back to earth—to Dad. He's waiting for us." He stared at his mother. "Mom, I don't understand. How did you get down there?"

She stared at him, confused. "What do you mean? You didn't take me?"

He cocked his head and raised his eyebrows. "No, I didn't." As one, they turned to Katie.

She stared at them and then bit her lip. "When that mean lady touched me, I was so scared I just wanted Mommy to come take me home." She turned to her mother and cuddled back against her. "When I imagined you, I found you and you came to me." She stared around her. "Danny, can we stay here? I like this place. It's like Magnolia Fields, only a million times better." Suddenly, she sucked in her breath and crinkled her brows. "Where's Charity?"

Danny shook his head. "I didn't take her with us. We left her down below."

Katie shivered despite the warm, humid temperature. "I didn't like that mean lady either," she said, hushed. "She was very, very bad."

Danny nodded, thinking about Marta. "As bad as it gets. But we're safe and I don't think either she or Charity will be able to bother us anymore."

Maddy spoke up. "Just how did you get us away?"

Danny shook his head. "I'm not entirely sure. So much of it is still a mystery to me. One moment we were being held by those creatures under Charity's control, and then something made her powers stop. The next thing I knew, you were there, getting shoved into that hole and all I thought about was trying to get you out. Do you remember what you saw down there, Mom?"

Maddy trembled slightly and then glanced at her daughter. Danny realized she didn't want to talk in front of her. "Let's just say I'm glad you got me out. And I think I know what stopped Charity's powers. When we found you all in the forest, we put your necklace on Charity. After that, the next thing I remembered was being below."

Michael sucked in his breath. "You must have dampened her abilities, Mom. That has to be it."

She nodded. "I think so, too."

Danny shook his head. "What I don't understand is why they needed Katie in the first place if Charity also had powers? It doesn't make any sense to me."

Michael looked at his mom. "Any guesses?"

"No, nothing I can think of." She looked away from them.

For some reason Danny felt a shiver run up his spine. He leaned over to his mother and held her hands in his. "Are you sure you're okay?"

She stared at him for just a moment and then smiled, rubbing his hair. "Yes, I'll be fine. I'm just a little shook up. That's all."

Danny breathed a sigh of relief. For a moment, his mother didn't seem right, but she looked better now. He stared at the ground. "Dad's freaking out. We have to go back."

"Then let's go," Michael said.

They all stood. Michael took Katie and cradled her tightly in his arms and she laid her head on his shoulder. Danny took his mother's hand, and then Michael's and closed his eyes and concentrated.

They disappeared.

Chapter Twenty-Three

Danny opened his eyes. He was so cold. He sat up and his father glanced at him. Relief was stamped on his features. "Thank God, you're waking up."

Katie was in her father's arms and she struggled against him. He patted her head. "It's okay, sweetie, you're safe."

"Where's Danny and Michael and Mommy? Where's Magnolia Fields? Where's the mean lady?" Danny lip-read as his sister started crying hysterically.

"The lady? Do you mean Charity? She can't bother you, honey, and your mom and brothers are right here next to you."

Maddy slowly sat up and brushed the snow from her cheeks.

"You all right, Maddy?"

She nodded and placed her hand to her temple as if she had a headache.

Danny moved next to her. "Mom, what is it?"

She stared at him vacantly for a moment and then blinked. "I'm okay, Danny. Jumping these worlds seems to take a bit out of me. I'm still a little disoriented."

He waited next to her until he was sure she was okay, and then turned to Charity, who lay in the snow next to them, unconscious.

Then she opened her eyes.

Gary threw Katie to the side, grabbed the gun and pointed it at Charity. "Don't you dare move," Gary ordered, standing over her.

"Don't hurt her!" Maddy screamed. She crawled through the snow towards him. She stopped, a startled expression on her face. "I mean, I don't think she can hurt us. Look, she's not even moving."

She was right. Charity was motionless, lying in the snow, her eyes open and unblinking. Flakes fell onto her face and she did nothing to remove them.

"Cuff her anyway, Dad," Michael said heatedly. He dug them out of the snow, where Gary had thrown them while Michael was unconscious.

Gary caught them and was ready to put them on the girl, but paused.

Maddy had moved next to Gary and stared at the young woman. She bent down to her and gently cradled her face with her hands.

"What in the world are you doing?" Gary asked.

Maddy frowned, holding Charity's chin in her hands and turned her face left and then right. Then she pinched the girl's arm and waved her palm across her eyes. Charity never moved. "She's completely unresponsive. It must have happened when she fell into the fissure."

"Fissure?" Gary asked.

Katie piped up. "She fell into the dark hole with the mean lady, Daddy. Michael pushed her in when the lady was fighting with Mommy."

He turned to Maddy, his mouth ajar. "You fought Marta? Please, someone has to tell me what's going on."

"Let's get inside and we'll tell you everything, Dad. Please, it's freezing out here," Danny suggested.

With that, Maddy picked up Katie, Gary picked up Charity and together they limped back to the bungalow to contact the authorities.

Chapter Twenty-Four

FBI agent Bob Daley came out of the observation room and rubbed his face with his hands. He stood outside the one-way mirror, watching two medical doctors speak to Katie and Danny. He turned towards Gary and Maddy. "It's amazing they're coming through this so well. They're both very strong kids, but I don't have to tell you that." He turned to Maddy. "Have you been able to remember what happened to you yet when you fell into the fissure?"

Maddy creased her brows. "Bob, it's like a miserable black hole in my memory. One second I was putting the necklace around Charity's neck in our reality and the next I was pulled down. I just remember feeling pain and this incredible despair. It's as bad as everyone thinks it is. It's dark, horrific and evil, and the worst place imaginable. I dropped into that black oil and it was as if my entire soul was consumed with hopelessness. I could feel Marta holding on to me, speaking to me, but she disappeared. Then absolutely nothing until I woke up in Danny's level fifteen." She absentmindedly rubbed her temple.

Gary touched her arm. "But now you have headaches, don't you? They're making you confused."

She turned to him, her eyes unfocused for a moment, and then they cleared. "Yes, they come and go. I won't lie. This has affected me, Gary. I get disoriented now, like I'm hearing things. The experience has left me with this overlying malaise as if the entire misery of that existence is still sitting deep in my gut. I feel a little… torn apart." She started to tear up.

He held her to him tight. "It's okay, honey. We'll deal with it. I'm sure the disorientation will go away soon. We'll work through it, together."

"I hope so," she whispered. "To think all this time Herrington had a daughter. How did we not know about her?"

"Because he kept her very well hidden," Daley said.

Gary sighed. "It's amazing. We knew this man, lived near him, traveled with him, and we never knew he had a child. They must have sent her away when she was very young."

Daley leaned over and picked up a stack of files from the table next to him and rifled through one. He pulled out a photograph of a beautiful little girl, no more than seven years of age. It was a prep school shot, with her sitting primly on a stool in her school uniform consisting of a white button blouse, blue vest, and pleated blue skirt. Black loafers with white bobby socks adorned her feet. She stared at the camera, smiling, but it was her eyes that stood out. Precocious ice blue peeked out of a face framed in a heap of blond ringlets.

"They did," Daley said. "She left home at the age of six to attend an elite boarding school in Europe. They changed her last name to Stevenson. Schooled her in everything from biochemistry, religion, and the law. In fact, she was one of the lawyers who came to visit Herrington over the years, and we found records she posed as both a psychiatrist and a nurse in the medical facility as well. She was quite a brilliant young woman."

Maddy glanced at Gary. "Just like her parents."

Gary huffed and turned to Daley. "I thought everyone who visited the prison was thoroughly checked."

Daley nodded. "They were and she cleared. We've now traced her personal history back to her childhood and Herrington had developed multiple identities for her, complete with birth certificates, IDs, and passports. We just never knew. Not to mention that damn can of mints they let him keep."

Gary shook his head. "A phone in his cell. Who would have ever believed that?"

Daley curled his lip. "The warden has been dismissed, as has every guard on the floor who regularly checked Herrington's room. Not that it matters. He's in solitary confinement. They won't even give him a scrap of toilet paper now without investigating it with a set of magnifiers."

"And what about the machine?" Maddy asked. Her hand absently rubbed her temple again.

Daley sighed. "We went back to check, Maddy. The machine Herrington had built, that you yourself examined all those years ago, is gone from the storage facility. We've gone back over tapes and logins for the past fifteen years and no one has been able to figure out when it was taken."

She dropped her hand. "So Charity must have taken the machine at some point."

Daley nodded. "Most likely, but I can't tell you when. She used that machine as a base and modified it. It will be waiting for you in the lab when you're ready to examine it."

One of the doctors in the observation room stood and left the room. Seconds later the door opened and he came in.

He nodded towards the children. "They're both doing incredibly well under the circumstances."

Maddy glanced at Gary and Daley as an unspoken message went between them. They had told the children they needed to keep what happened a secret. No one could know what really occurred. They had told the doctor that Charity had kidnapped their daughter and taken her into the woods before Danny and Michael found them. There was a fight, but Charity had some sort of convulsion and had been unresponsive ever since. At least, that was the story they were going with.

The doctor nodded. "I'll have them released immediately. Let me get their paperwork in order." He left the room.

When they were alone, Daley turned to Gary. "Have you been able to find out anything more from Katie? Why they wanted her in the first place?"

Gary shook his head. "All she's been able to tell us is that when she was pulled by Marta, she could feel part of her body fading away. That Marta was trying to eat her."

"Fading away? Trying to eat her?" Daley asked. "What does that mean?"

Maddy moved to the mirror and placed her hands on the surface. Then she leaned forwards and rested her head against it. "I know what they wanted her for," she said, quietly.

Gary came to stand by her side. "You do? Why haven't you told us?"

Maddy closed her eyes. "I was trying to figure out how to say it properly."

Maddy was quiet for a while when Gary prompted her again. "Honey, what did they want her for?"

She took a breath. "They wanted to use her. To have Marta jump into her body and bring her to the surface—to ride along the waves of her consciousness and use Katie to help her come back to life."

Gary was horrified. "Did they succeed?"

Maddy shook her head, her lips pinched. "No, they didn't. Katie's fine. Marta fell into the fissure and never made the switch."

"Thank God." Daley said, relieved. "Could you imagine having Marta in this world?"

"Forget that." Gary said. "Can you imagine her possessing my daughter?"

Daley glanced at them. "How about you guys go get Michael and I'll watch the kids while they get released. Michael's trying to be strong, but I imagine this entire thing has shaken him pretty bad."

Gary and Maddy nodded and left the room, moving across the hospital and into the psychiatric ward. They passed by a guard and through a series of locked doors. Arrows pointed them to room 354. Michael stood outside the room's window, staring inside it. His lower leg was bandaged and a pair of crutches leaned against the wall.

The guard posted outside the door nodded as they moved to the window and looked at the patient inside.

"She do anything yet, Michael?" Gary asked.

Michael shook his head. "Nothing, Dad. She's done nothing, but just lay there. No one knows what's wrong with her, but I do." He turned to his father. "She got past level fifteen, that's what I think. No way she can come back from that. I think her soul is stuck somewhere below and she can't come back to her body." He turned back to the window.

Charity lay in bed, catatonic. A doctor tried to talk to her, to check her reflexes, but the girl was unresponsive. The necklace Charity had given Danny was still snugly secured around her neck, exactly where Gary had told them to keep it.

Michael glanced at his parents. "Mom, you know the reason we got away is because you put the necklace on her. At that very moment Charity's powers weakened in our reality and since she was no longer in control of the beings, we were able to escape. It's when you showed up, too." He shuddered. "I can't believe I pushed her into that hole. I essentially killed her." He stared at his father, his eyes wide. "I could hear her screams as she fell. They went on and on. Right, Mom? Until the moment Danny took us away." He pulled back from the window and reached for his crutches. "Can we get out of here?"

Gary patted his shoulder and smiled. "Yeah, we can get out of here. Let's go."

Maddy turned to them. "You guys go on ahead and get the kids. Let me just talk to the doctor inside about something, okay?"

Gary nodded and he and Michael moved down the hall, disappearing through the security doors.

When she was sure they had gone, Maddy turned and walked into the observation room. She addressed the doctor, who wrote in Charity's file. "Do you mind if I remove her necklace? It was a gift she gave my son and he'd like it back."

The doctor nodded and turned back to his papers.

Maddy turned to Charity and unclasped the chain, removing it from around her neck. For a second she paused. She stared at the girl and then put out her hand tentatively, brushing a wayward curl off Charity's face and placing it behind her ear. With a shudder, Maddy put the chain quickly around her own neck and clasped it.

An audible sigh of relief escaped Maddy and she turned to the doctor. "Thank you." She left the room and went to find her family.

Epilogue

Inside a white-walled room, with no doors and no windows, stood a five-by-five, barred prison cell. Steel bars on all sides held a kneeling, screaming woman. Her blond hair was clumped and matted, her demeanor wild. Her emaciated body was nothing more than a skeleton and her ragged yellow dress barely covered her. She shrieked and pumped at the bars with her fists and continuously threw herself against them trying to get out. This prison cell had no doors, no locks and nothing to allow her to escape. It was a solitary cell in the middle of nowhere.

The woman stopped screaming and sniffed at the air. She sensed something and like a rabid animal began moving around the cell, smiling evilly. She gripped the bars with her two fists and leaned her face into the opening, which was only the width of her cheeks and stretched her bleeding lips so wide, her rotting teeth protruded. Her ice-blue eyes, the whites streaked with red, were suddenly lucid and she spoke in a voice so cold most would have nightmares for weeks just hearing it once.

"I'm still here. I'm not going away," she cooed maniacally. Her voice floated up and out through the bars to an unseen person. Up and out, oozing through the white walls, through thousands of miles of rock and dirt and filth, through skin and flesh and bone, until they came to rest on the surface.

Katie Anderson sat on the grass in the backyard of her home, feeding crumbs to an anthill. She watched the worker ants methodically bringing food nearly a hundred times bigger than themselves back to their nest to feed the babies and their queen.

A month had passed since the incident. Charity was locked up in a private psychiatric ward upstate, constantly guarded until she regained her psyche and could be put up for trial for the deaths of three people at the lab facility, for shooting Michael, and for abducting Katie.

At the prison, Herrington remained in solitary confinement. New charges were being brought against him for his involvement in Katie's kidnapping and the deaths of the guards at the facility. When they told Herrington that Charity had been caught and his attempt to find Marta had failed, he showed no emotion, although as they left, Herrington gave the slightest of smiles.

When they had turned back to ask him what was worth smiling about all he had said was, "Are you sure it failed?"

Katie took a small twig and pushed the crumbs around, breaking them apart into smaller pieces to make it easier for the workers to get their food. Her jacket was unzipped on this unusually warm November day. She glanced at their house. Danny was inside watching television and she could see her mom moving around in the kitchen. Michael was in the driveway with his father and she could hear banging as they worked on one of their many construction projects.

A rustling charge pulsed in the air and, for a second, Danny glanced away from the television set and turned towards Katie, a frown on his face. Katie paused, too, watching as her brother stood and walked to the patio window. He stared at her curiously. She waved to him and he cocked his head, but he seemed satisfied Katie was okay. He turned back to the show he was watching and sat back down.

At that same moment, Maddy stood in the kitchen and paused as she was mixing batter for a batch of cookies. Her vision flickered for just a moment and she shuddered.

"I'm still here, Maddy... I'm part of you now..." Marta crooned, locked in a cell in the dark recesses of Maddy's mind.

Maddy touched her necklace and squeezed the links so tightly her knuckles whitened. The dampening metals gave her that last added bit of control to hold Marta back. To hold back the woman who had made the jump from the underworld and was now residing in the far reaches of Maddy's consciousness.

Maddy took a deep breath. *"I know, Marta, but you won't be for long."*

"Don't be too sure," Marta hissed.

With a shiver, Maddy turned back to the batter and the rustle died away.

About the Author

Elyse Salpeter is the author of FLYING TO THE LIGHT, Book #1 in this series. She has also written an adult thriller called THE HUNT FOR XANADU, and a YA dark fantasy series with novels THE WORLD OF KAROV and THE RUBY AMULET. Elyse is married and lives on Long Island, NY with her twins. When she's not writing, she can usually be found dragging a 15-inch laptop up and down subway steps, just so she can have twenty minutes of free time to write on the train on her commute to work. Her groans can usually be heard for at least a five-block radius.

Please feel free to sign up for her newsletter here: http://www.elysesalpeter.com/contact.html

You can also follow her here:

Facebook: www.facebook.com/elysesalpeterauthor
Twitter: www.twitter.com/elysesalpeter
Web: www.elysesalpeter.com
Blog: www.elysesalpeter.wordpress.com

Want to read more from Elyse? Check out Book #1 in her YA Dark Fantasy series,

THE WORLD OF KAROV.

Chapter 1

It was the smell that woke me from my troubled dreams. That distinct, metallic scent of an animal when it's been run over by a wagon and left to die in its own filth on a dirt road riddled with the excrement of horses. Since this smell was in my room, it terrified me.

It was late; so late the hens were still fast asleep and the insects had ceased their incessant chattering for the night. Even the passing horse carts, which brought their furs and goods between the villages, had silenced and gone to bed for the evening, only to resume in a few hours to start their barter dance once again.

I couldn't bring myself to open my eyes, fearful of what I would find. I listened for my twelve-year-old brother's labored breathing, listening for the snores that accompanied my twin's dreams. I heard nothing and it meant only one thing. He was up and waiting for me to discover what he'd done. I could feel his anticipation like tingles on my skin; feel his eyes boring through the patched quilt as they tried to see how I'd react. I knew him like I knew myself because we were intrinsically linked by more than just this shared bedroom. We were linked by the bond of blood. We were identical twins and shared an unbreakable connection most twins did, but one which was horrible and twisted. We were as different as they came. My twin harbored a soul so mutated he couldn't be called human. He lived to cause misery to others and nothing made him happier than when he was bullying younger kids, hurting small animals, or stealing from the local merchants. He was the vandal who stole the poor farmer's eggs and smashed them on their houses for fun. He was the one the villagers' thoughts turned to when their beloved pets went missing and the one people feared so deeply they tried their best not to ever look him in the eye and cause him any reason to seek them out. They stayed silent through all their fears, knowing if they ever said anything, my brother would come to visit worse atrocities on them in retribution.

Gulping down my dread, I raised my arm and laid my hand gently on my chest. The sticky fur stuck to my palm and though I tried my best not to scream, to make any sound, I just couldn't stop it. A horrified moan escaped my lips and I opened my eyes. I could practically hear Alec giggling under the covers.

The moon chose that moment to come out from behind the clouds and illuminate the little stray lying across my chest. She had been choked with a piece of rope we used to tie up the goat in the backyard. Rivulets of congealed blood stained her delicate little nose. Wide brown eyes stared at me, wondering what she had possibly done to deserve this, wondering what in heaven's name could have possessed the boy who had taken her in and lovingly cared for her only days before, to turn against her. Although I knew the face she saw as she died was mine, she would possibly have had no idea it really wasn't me, but a terrible evil, which walked the land in my own likeness.

Shaking in anger, I bundled the cat together with my ruined blanket and sat up, holding it accusingly as I stared at the mound of covers that shook gleefully on the bed across the room from me.

"You didn't have to do this." My words fell on deaf ears. He wouldn't answer me, the same way he didn't answer me for any of the other hundred accusations I threw at him. How I hated him.

We should have been best friends and closer to each other than anyone else on this Earth, but we weren't. We had always been dirt poor, residing in a ramshackle three-room house replete with poorly patched holes in the walls from where my father had punched his fists through them from one violent fit or another. There was the requisite dilapidated barn and a patch of farmland long since gone to seed. My father occasionally sobered up just long enough to take the occasional odd job helping other farmers with their crops or herds, but those jobs came few and far between because the villagers were scared of him and his rantings when he had too much to drink. The job never lasted long and he usually was never asked back.

When my father fell into one of his weekly drunken stupors, the rest of the family became the targets of his irrational ale-fueled fury. Since we were little, Alec and I bore the brunt of his beatings, but they were most fierce when my mother would occasionally intervene. Then things would get ugly. My mother would always end these sessions cowering in the corner of the kitchen next to the kettle, that night's dinner remains scattered on the floor and a swollen cheek and black eye she'd have to hide from the villagers during the next week. I was old enough to know they recognized what was happening and still did nothing about it.

After each of his tantrums, I'd escape into the silence and peace of the forest, trying to understand why my father did what he did. Alec's reactions to my father's outbursts were drastically different. He'd leave the house for hours on end, sometimes disappearing all night. The next day we'd hear about some farm catching fire, or a new baby sheep being mysteriously killed.

Unfortunately, in my town, people always looked the other way and refused to become involved unless something was happening to them directly. They saw me as a smiling, happy twelve-year-old boy on the outside who always helped them with their packages, helped them find their lost animals, and the one who always did well at school. That is, when I wasn't staying home nursing a black eye or tanned backside, which would cause too many questions if anyone thought to speak up.

I could have blamed my mom for not stepping in more, but she was a simple, timid woman. I was told by the town gossips on more than one occasion she had married the first boy who paid her a compliment when she was only seventeen years old. After she had given birth to Alec and me only a year later, she tended house. My father, her prince, quickly went from shining knight to her worst nightmare, but by that time, she had nowhere to go and didn't have the guts to leave with her boys. Imagine if she had been brave enough to teach us there was more to life than potatoes and bread for dinner for weeks on end, or the end of a belt as a bedtime story?

Because of our upbringing, Alec had so much hate built inside him. He directed it at me, convincing himself I was the reason for all his problems. I was the first-born, and came out healthier, whereas Alec was smaller and sickly at birth. As we grew, I was always stronger and more coordinated, while Alec struggled with even little things. Games were hard for him because he simply couldn't keep up with the other kids who were bigger and faster. We were both deemed smart by our teacher, but Alec didn't have the attention span to sit down long enough to do our lessons and they were a torture for him. Don't ask what happened when the teacher sent home notes from school asking my parents to try to help him with his lessons. They were never good nights.

Making friends was nearly impossible for him, because he had a really horrible way of relating to people and as a result, no one ever played with him. So he channeled his frustration at me. Never did it cross Alec's mind that if our father had been loving and kind and had worked to provide for his family, perhaps our lives would have been better. Maybe had he been the father he should have been, helping us with our homework, playing ball in the backyard, anything, it would have changed things. Maybe if our mother had been stronger, things would have been different.

I stared back at the kitten. This was the fifth stray animal this year I'd taken in and nurtured back to health and the fifth one to come to an untimely death. I knew my days taking in strays were officially over.

Silently, I left the room and made my way out to the rear of the small barn. There was a small patch of garden I had planted with wildflowers and in the back of a spray of hollyhocks and cosmos, in the dark of night, I buried the little lost cat, who had done nothing more in this world but look for food, for love, and for someone to take care of her.

It mimicked my life, for that was all I wished for, too. A place to feel needed and loved. A place to feel accepted and safe. A place where I could be all I could be.

Just anywhere but here.

To read more, you can purchase THE WORLD OF KAROV here: http://amzn.to/WFJo3f

Printed in Great Britain
by Amazon

82410036R00119